THE
CROCODILE
GOD

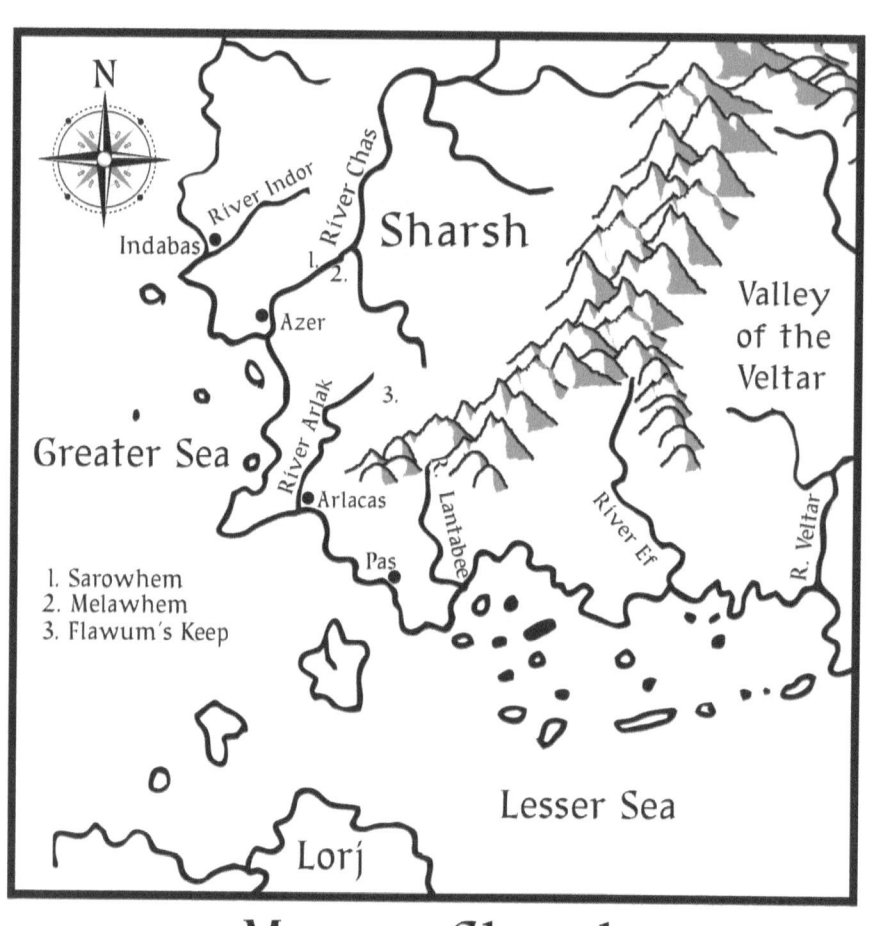

Muram Sharsh

The Crocodile God

Stephen Brooke

Arachis Press 2019

The gods can see in you what men may not.

The Crocodile God
©2019 Stephen Brooke

ISBN 978-1-937745-64-6

Arachis Press
4803 Peanut Road
Graceville, FL 32440
http://arachispress.com

Part I.
BROTHERS IN CHARMS

1.

"They have named the boy Saj, for his father."

"A good Muram name," stated Qala, "and a good Muram man."

The Sharshite nobleman shrugged. "I suppose. But they had best name the next one after his Uncle Corad."

"Unless it be a girl," his companion objected. A thought, a slight smile. "Then they might name her Lelanva."

Corad said nothing but appeared both puzzled and curious. "My true name, my birth name," the former pirate queen told him. "I have not used it in, ah, twenty years or more."

"I shall be certain to mention this in my next letter."

"No, no, best to just forget it," she objected. "I should have kept my mouth shut. Or filled it with more wine!"

Corad's answer was to refill her goblet. Qala appreciated the man's tact. It was one reason they remained friends, aye, had become closer friends over the past two years, despite the fact that he had once been chained in one of her galleys. His eyes went to the slender young woman standing at the door.

"Um, ma'am," she began. Her accent was of the south, and revealed her Ildin origins as much as her looks. "The young master's — friend visited again."

"Mong?"

"Yes, ma'am. He popped in for a couple minutes. I think his mama called him back."

Qala sighed. "I was warned their connection might grow stronger. Thank you, Samee." She nodded a dismissal to the girl.

Rather than ask the obvious questions, Corad remarked, "Zedos's nurse is rather pregnant, I see. It seems only a month or so since I attended her wedding."

She chuckled at her friend's jest. It had only been a month or so. Well, two months. Samee and Benaro had quite apparently not waited for the official rites. "I am sure they would have wedded sooner had not your sister wanted a double ceremony at Spring Feast." Qala suspected that Domi and Ranwif had waited. Or came closer to waiting, anyway.

She peered at her companion over the rim of her goblet. It was a serviceable goblet, unadorned, but of gold. "You are curious about my son's friend, aren't you?"

"I would guess it has something to do with your friendly gods," the noble replied. "Zedos's relatives."

"More or less. Mong is a mafadwi, one of the, uh, demons of their world. A very young one, of an age with Zedos."

"Ah, the changeling Mawa stole and tried to pass off as your son." Qala nodded. "And the reason its mother mistakenly grabbed Zedos and carried him back to her world." Corad had heard most of the story, and not just from her. Others would have their versions of it. For that matter, having been a part of it he would have his own version.

"*His* mother," Qala corrected him. "Mong never stays long but he has been appearing now and again, more frequently over the past couple months. They have some sort of bond."

Corad but lifted an eyebrow at this, remaining silent for some time, sipping his wine. Corad was ever one to sip, one to avoid excess. Qala was not sure she liked this about him. At last, "Have you spoken with any of the gods about this?"

"I've seen little of them since those times. None of them for months now." Qala, however, suspected they were keeping an eye on their nephew. "The first time Mong showed up, Budo came and told me not to worry about it."

"Budo. He's the brother I haven't met." Corad did not sound overly eager to remedy that.

"He pays more attention to what goes on with the mafadwi than the others." Big, honest, well-intentioned, but not overly-bright Budo — the one divine relative of Zedos she was willing to trust. That included the boy's father.

Wherever he might be. Was Xido yet a colossal crocodile, swimming the oceans? Qala had heard nothing, neither from mortal nor god. "You'll leave early?" she asked, desiring to turn the conversation elsewhere.

"There's no great hurry. I'll have plenty of time for a breakfast from Benaro. I hated turning him back over to you after his apprenticeship in our kitchens!"

"I was glad of the return of both apprentices I sent you. As were the girls who wed them."

"Yes, Ranwif. I think he would never have agreed to train as an equester at our house had not Benaro already been bound there." Face expressionless, voice even, he added, "He still greatly dislikes my father."

"With reason." That Lord Hurrum had played a role in the death of Ranwif's family — albeit a passive one — they both recognized. "But I think maybe your sister had more to do with his going."

His half-sister Domi, that was, a natural daughter of Hurrum. Not so long ago, neither would have mentioned the relationship. Domi now served as bailiff here at Melawhem, a rare position for a woman to hold. "Perhaps so," agreed Corad. "And now I shall take him away again for a little while."

"Oh, he travels to Flawum's court from time to time anyway. If —" She paused, frowned. "If your mission is successful, I fear he and Domi will leave me to live there."

Corad nodded. "As both an equester of the empire and a scion of the old Sharshite nobility, he is just the sort Flawum would want in his kingdom."

"So it is to be a kingdom?" asked Qala. That had been up in the air the last time they had spoken.

"Most likely. The Mura insisted that I first offer him the title of baron. He wouldn't go for it, of course, so now I'm authorized to agree to celos, which Flawum campaigned for from the start."

Celos. Muram for king. Qala's own name was a variant on the word in the dialect of her birthplace across the sea. "Celos of what realm?" she asked. "Not Sharsh, obviously."

"No, he must relinquish any claim on the Sharshite throne. Flawum will be the Pretender no longer." The nobleman seemed quite firm on that — as, no doubt, were his superiors. "Whatever his realm be called, he is claiming he should rule all the way from River Chas to the sea. That, I am sure, is but a bargaining position."

Qala grimaced. "That could include my own estate. I would rather it didn't." Not that she had anything against Flawum, but she was Muram, after all, and preferred to be ruled by the distant Muram emperor. So long as he remained distant. "You'd best do a good job as envoy, my friend!"

It would be good for trade in this part of the world — both their estates would profit from the roads south being opened again. Qala had been thinking for some time on how to best take advantage. She had old contacts down on the coast of the Lesser Sea, smugglers who might need to turn their hands now to honest commerce. They could be useful.

"Only the morrow will answer that." Corad laughed and slid his chair back. "But I'll keep you up no later tonight, my lady."

One of the rooms upstairs had been prepared for Corad. Those rooms were where the owners of the estate used to live. Qala herself preferred this suite on the ground floor, quarters once of the bailiff and his family. "I'll walk you up to your chamber," she said, rising. In Corad's own home, he would have called a servant for this task. Qala was used to doing things herself, preferred doing things herself. "Let me check on Zedos first."

"I'll say goodnight to the young master," spoke Corad, following her into the adjoining room. Zedos was playing quietly, pushing a painted wooden horse back and forth across the faded rug. Samee's own daughter slept in her mother's arms. The boy jumped up at once and ran to his mother. He might be small — and, as his parents, likely to remain so — but he was an active boy and had walked early.

He stopped suddenly and looked up at the pair with a most serious expression. "Go bye," he said. Then Zedos simply disappeared.

2.

"It does no good for you to remain here, my friend," said Qala. "You have duties in the south."

"Not pressing ones. I would not desert you." Corad was unlikely to change his mind. But it would, indeed, do no good for the Sharshite noble to stay on at Melawhem. He could not help her rescue Zedos this time, as he had done more than a year since.

There was nothing any of them could do. They had waited through the night for something, anything, to happen. Qala had little doubt that Zedos had somehow traveled — or been pulled, maybe — to the home of his father, a world of gods. It was nowhere for a boy of less than two years to be on his own.

"We can only wait," she replied. Weary she was, and frustrated. There was simply nothing she nor anyone else could do. Anyone mortal.

But she would not leave this room. Qala sat on the floor, a blanket pulled around her. If her son returned, it would be here, would it not? None the less, she had told Ranwif to have parties out patrolling the grounds in case the boy showed up elsewhere. A hint of dawn's light silhouetted a form at the front door. Domi, who had been coming and going with messages. Qala looked up at the girl. "Tell Benaro to bring something from the kitchens, will you? Or whoever is there at this hour," she spoke.

But the girl was not paying attention, not looking at her at all. Her eyes were fixed on something across the room and Qala turned to see a movement, a swirling, in the darkened far corner, coalescing into the form of a small, very dark woman. In her arms was Zedos.

A happy Zedos, it seemed, who laughed when she put him down, and ran to his mother. "Mawa," was all Qala could say for a moment, as she swept the boy up into her embrace. "I thank you."

Domi seemed dumbfounded. She had never seen any of Zedos's aunts and uncles appear so before. Not so for Corad. He appeared none too comfortable with the goddess' arrival but managed to greet her politely. "My lady."

Mawa nodded to the nobleman and looked about. "Nice rooms. You moved in last year, no?"

Though dozens of questions thrust themselves forward in her mind, Qala replied, "In the spring. They were made ready at last over the winter when there was little else that needed attention on the estate."

"Oh yes, you have winter here. I do detest cold weather." The goddess laughed at a sudden thought. "Perhaps my nephew shares my feelings and came to keep warm!"

"He was with Mong?"

"Indeed. His mother Ir at once sent word to Budo when he appeared, and he informed me." She regarded the little boy for a moment. Zedos had turned in his mother's arms and was regarding her in return, his dark eyes fixed on his divine relative. "He does not seem to share our double nature. It would have shown itself — we were as mafadwi when young and could not yet divide ourselves."

Qala was pleased to hear this but felt it best not to say so. "But he does share your ability to move between worlds."

"At least between your world and mine. Part of the boy is connected to the home of his father. Oh — Xido has returned."

So the god no longer swam the seas as a crocodile, mindless? "Has it been long?" The Muram woman was unsure whether she would have welcomed a visit, yet she felt he should have shown some interest in his offspring.

"A year and more in your world. We might have noted his arrival had we not been busy rescuing his son at the time."

"Perhaps not," spoke a voice from the shadows behind her. A compact black man stepped out of them. "Xido is good at being unobtrusive when he wishes."

"This is so," agreed Mawa. "He needed some time to sort through things, I think."

"I greet you, Lord Lenco," spoke Corad.

Mawa snickered. "Not even the mafadwi address my brother as lord."

"Maybe we should start a new custom," replied Lenco. "I greet you, Lord Corad. And you my ladies," he said to Qala and the dumbfounded Domi. This latter managed something resembling a curtsy.

"Go on to Benaro now," her mistress told her, "and get that breakfast for us. Will you stay?" she asked the deities.

Lenco looked like he might be willing but Mawa spoke up. "We'd best be home." Domi nodded and scurried out.

"I'll need to be on my way, as well," said Corad. He gave the pair of gods a glance and added, "I'll grab something in the kitchen and be on the road to Flawum."

Lenco and Mawa exchanged an enigmatic look. "How fares the young king?" asked the goddess.

"Well indeed," the Sharshite told her. "A changed man. Marriage and new-born twin daughters have something to do with that, I would think."

Not to mention a short sojourn in these gods' world, Qala added to herself. More looks between the sibling gods. "Then fare you well, Corad," spoke Mawa. "Give our greetings to him."

The nobleman bowed to Qala and slipped out the door. "It would be best Flawum not know he has children in our world too," said Lenco. He snickered, giving his sister a sidelong look. "Fortunately, none with Mawa."

He would probably not have survived had Mawa the Spider mated with him, Qala knew. She had a habit of devouring her lovers. Her male lovers. One should never forget that this slender pair of human-seeming individuals were also strange and powerful deities. "The mafadwi with whom he coupled?" she asked.

"All three," came Mawa's reply. "As with us, they can choose whether to conceive."

So Mong would have another sibling back in his mother's cave. One fathered by a mortal man — albeit a mortal with gods in his own family tree. "We would rather they had not," added her brother, shrugging. "It was necessary to compromise at the time, I suppose."

"Yes, I made a deal. What will come of it will come of it." Mawa lifted her eyes toward the doorway. "Your Domi returns and we shall leave," she said, stepping back into the shadows, which swirled about her.

Lenco bowed and followed.

3.

It would not do to appoint one of these as her master of arms, should Ranwif leave her service. Qala stood in her doorway, surveying the three ex-pirates who served her, the men who jokingly called themselves her 'crew.' No, they were able enough men and two had even taken women since settling in at her estate, but she should have a Sharshite in charge of security at Melawhem. One with the rank of equester, maybe.

"Anything to report, Babo?" The Baxac man had been Ranwif's official second almost from the beginning. This was a matter of politics — the other two were Mura, and Qala did not wish her tenants to think she favored her own people over Sharshites. That Babo was the most competent was a bonus.

"All most quiet, my lady," he responded. "Two traders come up road this morning. Maybe some we see not too."

"From the south?" All such would have hidden their passage not so long ago.

"So it is. Nothing much on river either."

Bandy-legged Sorg piped up. "Lumber rafts goin' downstream, mostly."

It was too early yet for much else, with Summer Feast still a month away. She should confer with Domi about the celebrations soon.

And about Zedos's second birthday coming later that summer. Plenty of time yet to plan for that. Sharshites celebrated birthdays and she intended the boy to grow up as a Sharshite aristocrat. Even if he had not a drop of Sharshite blood in him!

"Very well. Patrol as you see fit and keep an eye to the south. Augun, you remain with me today." The burly one-eyed pirate nodded. He was used to serving as Qala's personal guard and sometime fencing partner. Their mistress watched for a moment as the other two meandered off. "They are happy here," she said. "How about you, Augun?"

The big man shrugged. "There be worse places."

Qala had to laugh at that. "Far worse. But you were mate of a vessel before. This must seem a step down." Not that the fellow had the brains to have ever risen any higher in the pirate fleet.

"I do not miss those days, Qala," replied Augun, and no more.

"Neither do I," she said. Ah, but he missed other things, she knew. His lover Lovi, chief cook at Lord Hurrum's estate, for one. It had taken her a while to recognize why the former pirate always asked to accompany her to Sarowhem. Babo and Sorg had known, of course.

So had Corad, who only laughed when she mentioned her discovery. Sharshites tended to be more tolerant of such things than her own people. She should find some way to let them be together more, assuming the relationship lasted. Ha, here she was again helping all those about her find love but having none of her own. Only Zedos did she have. Only her son.

She would have spoken further with Mawa and Lenco, asked them if there were some way to prevent little Zedos from wandering, had they not left so abruptly. So happy was she simply with his return that such questions had not come to her at once. Qala would remember them next time.

Augun had stood quietly, patiently, through her reverie. He knows my moods, she told herself. "Watch the door a while," she said. She would spend some time with that son before turning to the business of the day.

He nodded and then looked past her. "Someone comes."

A horseman, and one in a hurry. He did not dismount but sat his steed before her porch. "Lady Qala?" the man asked. A Sharshite man he was, and in the colors of Flawum, red and gold. The old colors of Sharsh — he might need to change them when things were worked out with the empire.

"I am Qala," she stated, taking one step forward.

"I bear news of Lord Corad," the messenger said. "He and his party were set upon while traveling south." The slightest of pauses, then, "None were slain but Corad received wounds. He rests now at our lord's keep."

Qala digested all this quickly. Corad was safe, good, and Ranwif as well. "You will carry this news on to his father? Or shall I dispatch someone?"

"I was charged to go to Lord Hurrum," came the response.

"Very well. Augun, escort the man across the river." She looked up again. "If you need rest or refreshment, the village inn will serve you. See to it," she said to Augun.

"Yes, my lady."

Her guard began to move toward the rider, who wheeled his horse about. "Wait. Better you go with him," she told Augun. "Ride to Sarowhem and return when you think best." He bowed and both headed toward the river and the ferry.

There was obviously more to this courier's story. He would lay it out in detail to Lord Hurrum, and Augun might or might not learn some things to tell her on his return. Either way, he could spend a little time with Lovi.

Who would attack Corad? She watched the two for a moment more and turned to enter her home. It was what, eight days since the morning he had left? The morning Zedos had been returned to her. There had been no more strange happenings with the boy since, nor had Mong visited.

There were undoubtedly factions on both sides that did not wish the nobleman's mission to succeed. Sharshite loyalists who saw Flawum's overtures to the Muram Empire as betrayal, treason. Mura who saw treating with the Pretender in much the same light, and would rather invade — and perhaps profit from it — than make peace. There might be others, too, including her own old friends and associates among the pirates and smugglers who preferred a lawless southland.

None of that would Qala figure out. Corad lived and he would continue the negotiations. She had more pressing concerns right here, an estate to run and a son to raise. That was quite enough.

4.

"His birthday is but a week before the Feast of Plenty. We could combine the celebrations," suggested Domi.

"No. Zedos needs his own day and his own celebration." It would not do to combine them. Not that the boy was likely to remember this one but it was best to set a proper precedent.

Domi gave an amiable nod. "There is yet plenty of time. We do need to make plans for Summer Feast."

She has completely shed her country manner of speech, thought Qala, over these past two years. The natural daughter of Lord Hurrum was moving up in the world, in a position of authority here, married to an aristocrat. An aristocrat of sorts. Why, if they ended up in Flawum's court, she would probably be addressed as Lady Domi.

"A bonfire, I assume," Qala said. "I thought it was too close to the barns last year."

"Maybe down by the river?"

"Hmm, yes. Pick a spot." Perhaps a permanent one. They could take that up later. "Any business we need discuss this morn?"

"No, my lady. All is well. The ground nuts are in bloom and the maize is more than waist-high."

"Good. Plenty of fodder for the swine this year, then?" The girl nodded. "We can spare a couple for the festival I am sure. Two steers too, maybe?"

"That should be enough," agreed Domi. It was her duty to be parsimonious when the lady of the manor would tend toward generosity. It had taken a while for both to settle into these roles which, Qala recognized, went against their actual natures.

"We," began her bailiff, "um, you should choose a replacement for Samee."

"Replacement?" Was her son's nurse going somewhere? Why hadn't she been informed?

"She'll be giving birth soon," Domi reminded her. "You'll need someone else for at least a couple weeks."

Oh, of course. "It should be someone young enough to chase after

Zedos," said Qala, "and not be too perturbed if Mong visits. That's one thing I like about Samee. She's never let it bother her."

"That is so," the younger woman conceded, perhaps with the least trace of reluctance, and then smiled. "She expected us to be strange sorts here in the north." Qala knew well that Samee and Domi were not close, despite spending much time together, despite their husbands being best of friends. "I'll ask around." She took her leave, off to attend to the many duties of a bailiff on a prosperous estate. It was an estate of middling size, just small enough she could give every aspect of its management some of her personal attention. Domi did so well, Qala knew.

She would miss her when she left — and yes, she was sure to leave, in time. The girl would be far more difficult to replace than Samee. But Samee was still with her today, in the nursery with Zedos and her own little girl. Oeletta was of an age with Zedos and his sometime playmate. She had even played with Mong when he visited.

Oeletta — that was a Sharshic version of the Ildin name her mother had given her. Best the girl grow up Sharshite. Everyone called her Letta, anyway.

The little one didn't look particularly Ildin, and promised to be sturdier of build than her mother. Samee had been reticent to speak of Letta's father but in time Qala had been able to piece together that he was one of Flawum's soldiers. Whether he was dead or had but abandoned her, she did not know. Nor did it matter now. She had a good husband in Benaro.

Qala stood a while in the doorway, watching the children, before turning her eyes to their nurse, quietly sewing in a chair. Samee must have weeks yet before giving birth, she felt. The pregnancy just showed up so prominently because the girl was such a scrawny little thing. Not unlike her mistress! Qala knew well of her own appearance while carrying Zedos.

"We should take the children outside later," she said. "It is a fine day. A warm day."

"Yes, m'lady," answered Samee. "It's a good thing they're big enough we needn't to carry them now."

16

Qala thoroughly agreed. "The child you're carrying now is quite enough, I would think. Hmm, are you up to walking very far?"

"Oh, yes, m'lady." Samee rose to her feet without too much difficulty, perhaps to prove it. "At least as far as the kitchen, where I am sure my husband could find treats for both the children and us."

"He spoils them," complained Qala, sounding not at all serious about it. "You both do."

The girl shrugged. "We both grew up poor. We want them to remember childhood fondly."

Qala resisted the temptation to tell her that her own childhood had undoubtedly been far worse, in slums on the far shores of the Great Sea. "Shall we go for a walk?" she asked the children.

Letta at once jumped up. "Want Daddy," She declared. The little girl had obviously been paying attention to the conversation. Women old and young had assured Qala that girls tended to be better with words when they were little. The one-time Pirate Queen accepted this, having no experience with children. They had simply not been a part of her life until now.

Oh, she did remember another life, before going to sea. She remembered sisters and brothers and playmates in a gray, bleak city. The faces and names had faded; they were but a dream to her now.

"Daddy you shall have," she assured Letta, and then noted Zedos staring at her, far too thoughtfully for one so young, she felt.

"My daddy gum," he said. The lad rose to join them without further words.

It was no great distance from her rooms to the kitchens. They need not even have stepped outside, but Qala would have none of that. They all needed exercise and fresh air. She wondered about her son's statement as they ambled toward the river. Zedos had never said a word about his father — or a father — before. Was it only a matter of growing awareness, of curiosity?

Or did the boy actually know something? He was the son of a god, after all, and had already shown unusual capabilities. Qala had no illusions that rearing a demigod would be easy.

Not that any children, it seemed, were easy to rear. Their path was lined with head-high mulberry trees. One of her first acts on taking possession of the estate had been to plant them. There was no reason they could not get in on the silk-producing trade here. It was a major industry not so far south; much silk was exported by Flawum's people. That would be easier for them to do, now, if Corad's negotiations worked out. No more need to smuggle it out.

She liked the berries, too.

The River Chas flowed at a normal level now, no longer the swollen flood of springtime. Still, it was a mighty river. She should get herself and her little sailboat out onto it soon. And why not Zedos, as well? It was time he became acquainted with boats. The boy stood beside his mother, one hand on her leg, staring at the water. Letta seemed quite uninterested and had plopped down on the lawn to play with one of the dandelions.

"That is the Chas," Qala told him. "Can you say Chas?"

"Tas," he responded. "My riffer." With that he let loose of his mother and ran toward the water.

"Stop!" Qala cried. "Don't, Zedos!" She ran after him. Samee snatched up her daughter and tried to follow.

No use. The little boy headed straight to the river bank and jumped in.

5.

Qala gazed, astonished, as her son paddled back and forth in the Chas's flow. Samee came up beside her, Letta in her arms. The young woman had shrieked quite loudly when Zedos plummeted over the bank. Now she watched too, no less amazed than the boy's mother.

But both knew he was a most unusual child. Was his father not a crocodile god? Qala asked herself. Perhaps she should have been expecting something like this. "Come out, Zedos," she called. "Let's go visit Benaro." She scrambled down the sandy bank, not too high here, and the laughing boy paddled to her. Qala lifted him out of the water and set him atop the embankment, none the worse for his escapade, aside from his dripping tunic.

"You mustn't do that without asking," she scolded, climbing up beside him. What if Chas had been in flood? The boy might have been swept away. "Now run around a while and get dry."

Qala could stand to dry off some herself. Her gown was wet up to the knees, and covered with sand somewhat higher. She should have worn a kilt; her people here were used to seeing her dressed so. As she wrung out the hem, she noted a man hurrying toward them. Augun it was.

"It's Lord Corad," he reported, as soon as in earshot. "And Ranwif. They just rode in."

"In the stables now?" she guessed. They were the sort of men who would see to their steeds first and themselves after.

"So they are," said the burly Mur.

"Tell them to come to us in the kitchens," Qala told him. "I need food and drink after this." The big man took in her disheveled state but asked no questions.

"Yes, my lady," he said, and headed back.

Augun had not been able to tell her much after accompanying Flawum's man to Lord Hurrum's estate. The messenger had closeted with the thegn and returned immediately. One bit of information the former pirate did glean when conversing with the fellow on their ride back, and that was that the attackers were a mixed group of men, not exclusively Mura nor Sharshites. That suggested they were smugglers or pirates, unhappy with this threat to their trade.

Also, Augun had informed her, there were rumors around Sarowhem of strange men skulking in the neighborhood. Qala had heard similar reports recently from her own people. Lovi had proven reluctant to speak of this to his lover, though he was usually full of gossip.

Qala's three companions were napping by the time Corad reached them. She herself was on a second tumbler of freshly brewed ale and feeling a desire to join them in slumber. The Sharshite nobleman — showing no outward signs of having recently been wounded — slipped in quietly, followed by young Ranwif. The latter gave a little bow to his mistress and went off to gossip with Benaro.

"So that is done," said Corad, taking a seat across the pine table from Qala. "How fare things with you, my lady?" He glanced toward the sleeping Zedos. Someone must have told him something of what happened. Augun, maybe.

"Well enough," she answered. "It seems my son is being true to his crocodile heritage."

"It's not a bad thing for a boy living on the banks of the Chas to know how to swim," said her companion. A girl brought him ale in an earthenware cup. "Thank you," he murmured, and went on. "I learned when not much older than Zedos."

"Your sister bathes in the river on warm mornings," noted Qala. "I prefer to be in a boat myself. So — how go things in the south?"

"A settlement has been worked out. Mostly worked out. I shall need escort a Muram ambassador south to finalize it all." He sipped his ale approvingly. "In a while. There is no great rush on any of it."

Qala chuckled. "Not on your side. Flawum may feel differently."

Corad answered soberly. "Perhaps, but he knows things can not be hurried."

"Is it all secret or can you tell me what is decided?" She tried not to sound overly serious with her question, though she burned to know the details.

"We have agreed his realm is to be bounded by the Arlak to the west and the mountains to the east. That gives him control of the roads to the Lesser Sea, which was his greatest concern."

That it did not include any land west of the river mattered little, Qala

20

knew. Much of that, especially in the Arlak's upper reaches, was lost in impassible swampland. "But north and south?" she asked.

"Flawum calls for thirty leagues north from his keep in the hills but may well settle for twenty. We shall see. Either way, his borders will be far from Melawhem."

"As long as I am not inside those borders, it matters little to me."

Corad nodded, understanding her feelings there. "We are willing to concede more to him in the south. He is to have the harbor at Arlacas." Only the Mura called it that. To the rest of the world, the town was Arlak-Port.

"Not the best of harbors," Qala pointed out. The river mouth was shallow and swampy. It was not really a good spot for a town, either, especially in the mosquito season.

"Most of the trade goes further east. The legitimate trade. We know well the smugglers who dealt with Flawum used the Arlak, so it won't hurt to allow him legal access to the sea. Indeed, it should help curb the lawlessness of the southern coasts." He leaned forward and informed her, almost as if imparting a secret, "It is agreed that his domain will be known as Cel Arlacana."

The Kingdom of the Arlak — a good enough name, felt Qala. "With the emperor's approval."

"His advisers seem to be in favor. And the viceroy — he may matter the most."

"Hmm, I'll put in a good word to him if I get to Indabas." Qala had done business with — and paid bribes to — the man in the old days. Corad might not know that but he wasn't likely to be surprised by it either. "Ah, you're awake again, Samee."

Barely. The girl stared for a moment at Corad. "Why don't you go tell your husband to bring something hot for Lord Corad? He's in the back wasting time with Ranwif, I suspect."

"Yes, m'lady," she said, and went off to find Benaro. The children slept on, shoulder to shoulder on a bench by the wall.

"Will you stay for Summer Feast?" asked Qala. "Or return?"

Corad shook his head. "The Lady Vasema would not forgive me."

"So bring Sesa here. Domi would love to see her."

"Perhaps when all these negotiations are done." A serving girl appeared with a plate for Corad. There was no sign of Samee. "There is still danger or I might even take my wife to visit Flawum. What have we here? Ah, Benaro learned his craft well in our kitchens!" He sniffed extravagantly at the aroma arising from the plate.

It was but a slice of ham and some corn cakes, Qala noted, country fare. But allow Corad his little flights of fancy. "Dangers? I suppose you will wish to borrow Ranwif again when you return."

"And take more men at arms than previously. It would not do for the ambassador to be slain. It would not do at all."

With that, Qala was in complete agreement.

6.

Summer Feast came and went. The crops grew taller. Fruit ripened. Samee's belly grew astoundingly big.

"It's time Damana took over," Qala decided. Benaro's younger sister already been helping Samee and seemed competent enough. Qala did think her a bit flighty. She hoped she could handle Zedos on her own.

Ah, the boy's second birthday was nearing. They should celebrate little Oeletta's too. Samee said the birth had come the day of the Feast of Plenty. She had been peeved at the time that she would miss the festivities but had since decided it was a propitious date for a birth. Surely, Letta would always have plenty! The new child, be it girl or boy, was likely to be born somewhat before then. Any day now, in fact.

Samee had sat waiting while these thoughts ran through Qala's head. "Should I go home then, m'lady?" she asked.

"Wherever you are most comfortable," Qala replied. "You know I gave birth to Zedos in the chambers you and your husband now occupy." Of course she knew it. Qala felt foolish for saying it as soon as it came out.

"Yes, m'lady." The girl seemed to hesitate. "Benaro would like me to go to his family's cabin."

The ancestral hovel, Qala thought but did not say. She did not much approve of the idea. Being mistress of Melawhem was as much a balancing act as ruling over pirates. One must know when to assert authority and when to step back. On this occasion, stepping back seemed the better choice. "Will the midwife be near?" she asked.

The girl nodded. "She lives close by." That was good. But it was not the nearness of the midwife that really concerned Qala. It was her own nearness. Qala had brought Samee here and felt protective of her, felt a bond. The girl was going elsewhere to have her child.

"Then it seems a good place for you to go," she said. "Now where are Damana and the children? Oh, you will let Letta stay here, won't you?"

"It might be best," Samee agreed. "I don't think my mother-in-law much likes having her about."

Qala both understood and disapproved. She also understood there was nothing to be done about it. Now where were the children? Damana should have brought them back inside by now. It was just like her to wander off somewhere with them and forget the time. Especially if there were boys about.

At least she didn't seem bothered by Mong's visits. Those had grown more frequent lately, after tapering off some following Zedos's disappearance. Qala suspected someone in the little monster's world had been keeping him at home. Maybe one of the gods, maybe his mother. She went to the door and looked out, but they were not to be seen.

"Thedoth?" came a voice from behind her. Qala turned to see Mong standing in the middle of the room. The young mafadwi had grown. He had always been larger than Zedos and now stood maybe a head taller. And what a head it was, with little horns beginning to bud from it! He looked less human all the time and more like the beast that was the other side of his nature.

"Zedos is playing outside," Samee informed him. Mong seemed perplexed, a frown creasing his little brown brow. He had not yet stepped outdoors in this world. Perhaps his mother had warned him against it.

"Thtay in cave," he decided and sat down on a rug.

"This is a house," Qala told him. "It is different from your mother's cave."

Mong tried it out. "Houth." He looked around before deciding, "Cave more good."

Ir's cave was a rather splendid place, Qala had to agree, with its luminous crystal walls. Everything in that world of the gods seemed more intense, even awe-inspiring, than here.

The mafadwi was staring at Samee. "Letta thithter?" he asked.

The girl laughed at the question. "Or brother."

He nodded. "Thedoth brother me. Milk brother."

Samee turned a questioning eye toward her mistress. "The two suckled together at the breasts of Ir," she told her. "This is why they have a bond." In part, at least. Qala suspected it was more complex than that and might involve Zedos's paternity.

"Have thithter," Mong informed them. His voice was quite grave. "Jong."

Flawum's daughter. If Mafadwi had a gestation period similar to humans, the child should be about a year old.

"Bring her to visit sometime, deary," said Samee. This, Qala did not think at all a good idea.

"No come," the mafadwi child responded. "Thtuck."

"She has no bond to this world," explained Qala. At least, that was what she assumed. But if the girl's father was here — well, Qala had to admit she didn't know enough. Even the gods seemed to make guesses about this sort of thing.

She looked at the mafadwi boy, whose attention had turned to Zedos's scattered toys. Mong was examining one of the wooden soldiers dear to his 'milk brother.' He reminded Qala of a mafadwi she had met at the cave of Budo, the male who had found a human woman to suckle her son. "Do you know Xonxon?" she asked.

Mong bared his sharp little teeth in a wide smile. "Thonthon daddy!"

Ah. Qala knew nothing of mafadwi mating customs but apparently they had not prevented Ir from having a baby with Flawum. Maybe the man's divine ancestry had been too much of a temptation for her. Yet if mafadwi could choose to conceive, Ir must also have seen something worthwhile in the horned Xonxon.

At that moment, the children burst into the room, their young nurse trailing behind. "Mongy!" called out Letta, as both little ones rushed to greet their friend.

Mong rose from his seat on the floor. "Go cave," he proclaimed, taking Zedos and Letta's hands in his own.

Samee grasped at once what the mafadwi intended. "Oh no, you don't!" she cried, snatching up her daughter. Damana, perhaps not fully understanding but recognizing something was going on, grabbed the free hand of Zedos.

Too late. Mong and the little boy both disappeared into a swirling of the air. A moment later, the teenage girl was drawn into it behind them.

Samee stared at the empty space. "Benaro's mother is not going to like this at all," she said.

7.

Qala's first thought was of Damana. If they had gone to Ir's cave, Zedos should be safe. Not that she wouldn't worry about him! But the girl — how might the mafadwi react to her presence? Qala knew Ir and her friends were entirely likely to eat humans. So she had been told and so she was willing to believe.

There was nothing she could do about any of it, absolutely nothing. Benaro should be told of his sister, though, and better she do it than Samee. "Wait and watch," she told the girl. "I'm going to talk to your husband."

The best hope was that Damana would pop back into this world on her own, and quickly. Sooner of later she would. She was tethered here. She did not belong in that other world. The mafadwi might think of that and realize she would not make a decent meal. Her substance would all return here.

Or they might eat first and think later. Some of them did not seem overly bright. Qala followed the central hallway of her manor house down to the high-ceilinged dining hall, and passed through it to the kitchens. When she had taken possession here, the hall had been long unused by any but spiders, and littered with trash. It did not rival the great hall at Thegn Hurrum's estate but Qala was proud of it now. She was proud of all she had done to make her home once more a fit place for herself and all those who lived and worked here.

Her chief cook was busy supervising his pair of assistants, preparing lunch for all who served in and around the manor house. She waved him to her, almost casually, trying to appear calm before the servants. The situation was explained simply. Qala avoided making mention of the many dangers she could imagine.

Benaro, of course, knew all about Mong and about Zedos visiting another world. Samee would have gossiped of such things to her husband. So all of this was not something completely new to him; he nodded without much expression through her explanations and turned back to his work when she finished. He was sauteeing onions as Qala left, and promising to send her lunch along shortly.

It was not to be supposed he told no one of it. Within an hour Domi and Ranwif were with her, displaying far more curiosity and concern. Qala could understand why Benaro would turn things over to the pair of them.

They had greater knowledge of the situation and of the dangers — Ranwif in particular, who had some personal experience of the gods. "They seem a randy bunch," he said. "Will the girl be, um, safe with them?"

Both Samee and his wife looked him askance. Damana had not exactly guarded her virtue in this world. Qala had to consider the question for a moment or two, thinking on all the things Mawa and Lenco and other deities had told her. "I think she *can* get pregnant there. It would be just like when I ate food in the world of the gods. It became part of me." Yes, that sounded right. She was pretty sure of it. "But I don't think a man from here could get a woman, um, a female pregnant over there. His seed would come back to this world with all the rest of him." Flawum had been a special case, thanks to having a god somewhere in his heritage.

But had not Budo said something about Xido choosing to give her a child? Did male gods — and maybe mafadwi as well — have such an ability, to make a conscious choice, even as the females? Maybe she could ask Mawa. Qala hoped she would bring Zedos home.

They waited still as evening came, and through the night. Qala started suddenly, realizing she had drifted into sleep. Samee was awake, holding Letta, who was not. Domi and Ranwif? Oh, they were at the door, peering out into the dawn.

"Mommy!" All four turned to see Zedos standing in the middle of the room. Alone.

Qala knelt and took the boy in her arms. "Where is Damana?" she asked him.

"Ungle Boo!"

"What's an ungleboo?" whispered Domi.

"Uncle," replied Samee. "I think he is saying uncle."

"Oh! Of course," Qala said. "His Uncle Budo. Is that where Damana is?"

Zedos nodded his head vigorously. "Damana like Ungle Boo."

"I hope Ungle Boo doesn't like Damana too much," observed Ranwif.

Qala stood, shrugged. "That will be as it will, won't it? At least she is safe with him until she is pulled back to us." No one or thing would eat the girl while she was in Budo's cave.

"Oh dear," said Samee, of a sudden. "I do believe I am having contractions."

Domi was immediately in charge. "Can you make it to Benaro's house?" she asked.

"I'm pretty sure," Samee replied, smiling weakly. "Or I can just drop it along the way."

"Then let's go. Ranwif, run tell her husband."

"Oeletta?"

"I'll watch her," promised Qala. The little girl was still fast asleep. In fact, so was Zedos who had drifted off as soon as Qala put him down.

"At least," said Samee, "this will keep Damana's mother so busy she may not even know the girl is missing."

"You couldn't have planned it better," Domi told her.

8.

"And still no sign of the girl?" asked Corad.

Qala shook her head. "I've no idea how long it might take. I spent nearly three days in the world of Krat and was not pulled back here."

"Krat? Is that the name of the place?"

"That's the head god. Father to Xido and all the rest of them. He's gone missing for centuries. Or millennia maybe. Nat," she called to the innkeeper, "bring some more wine, will you?" She snickered and added, "Put it on Lord Corad's tab."

Qala, of course, owned this inn across the river from her manor house.

"And the mother hasn't noticed yet?" Corad took the tumbler of red the innkeeper handed him.

"She may be wondering by now but she has a new grandson to demand most of her attention. Good healthy boy — I don't know how such a big baby came out of such a little girl!"

"One might have said the same of you." He drank deeply, more deeply than was normal for the man. "The ambassador had better hurry along or we shall both be too drunk to greet him."

"That might be to the good," felt Qala. "Who are they sending, anyway?"

"An old friend of yours," replied the nobleman, who actually winked before continuing. "Admiral Murgom."

He has had too much to drink, thought Qala. But Murgom — "The admiral does know how things are in the south," she noted. She also wondered if she could pass Zedos off as his son. Murgom had notoriously poor eyesight.

No, best not to chance it. Nor to renew her relationship with the man.

"He's as knowledgeable about the situation as anyone," admitted Corad. "Speaking of the south, a new letter from my sister has arrived."

"All is well?"

"Saj is prospering. He has already become one of the wealthier men in Lanlaz. Marana says he would been asked to serve on the council were he a little older."

"He might as well aim for Lord Mayor."

"Give him time." Qala raised her mug to that, as did Corad before going on. "Our old friend Captain Nedos has resigned his position in Nota."

As second to the Muram military governor there, the *dux*. "It was a good post," she said. "It could have been a stepping stone."

Corad shrugged. "Being Sharshite would always have held him back, despite his Muram citizenship. He remains in Nota but is now in business — and partners with Saj on a couple ships."

"He married, didn't he? A local girl." Corad had mentioned this before.

"Ildin, but not local. It seems my sister and her husband had some sort of adventure in the interior and brought her back with them. Marana is not willing to give many details." He stared into space, musing for a moment before going on. "Um, they might have encountered Zedos's father, from what Nedos has said. He writes my father sometimes, you know." Nedos was more a friend of Lord Hurrum than of his son.

"Xit?" He was on Lorj?

"A gigantic crocodile aided them against a pirate fleet. We can make what we will of that." Both sat silently for a moment, doing just that. "It is rumored the new king of the pirates has moved their base to Lorj," Corad continued.

"Not a bad idea," admitted Qala. "It *will* bring them into conflict with the Baxac corsairs of the south."

"Let us hope they do not join forces. Do you know this new Pirate King?"

As their leader up until near three years ago, Qala had been familiar with all the important pirate captains. "Probably. Have you a name for him?"

Corad only shook his head. Tom the stable man rushed in at that moment. "Horses comin' up the road!" he announced. "Lots of 'em."

"The ambassador, no doubt. Old Murgom's taken his time," said Qala.

"He needs ride in a litter. Murgom is no horseman."

"Perhaps I should have gone down to Sarowhem and fetched him back in my boat. Ho, Tom," she called. "Will you run to the ferry and tell them to be ready? It will take many trips across Chas, I fear."

"You'll want a bigger barge if trade from the south picks up," observed Corad.

"A second one of the same size might prove more practical. Shall we go out and greet my guests?"

It was a large party. Qala was fairly certain she could fit them all in somewhere. If not, some could camp. They'd be doing that all the way to Flawum's keep, after all. Lancers at the fore, ten of them, and all Mura. More she spied at the rear of the column, probably another ten, as a typical Muram troop was made up of twenty men. Afoot, attendants and soldiers. Pack horses were led. Two horse litters — who might be in the second? Murgom hadn't brought his mistress along, had he? Qala had somewhat fond memories of time spent with the woman. She wondered if the admiral knew of them.

A man on horseback rode beside one of the litters. "Why, that is Vullum, isn't it?" she whispered to Corad.

"My father-in-law is to advise the admiral in the final negotiations," the nobleman responded. "And he brought along Sesa's mother." He sighed. "I hoped she might remain at Sarowhem."

The Lady Galana? That forceful woman had probably demanded to accompany her husband. "Your parents are undoubtedly grateful she did not."

Corad stifled his laughter and went to greet the admiral. He was as Qala remembered him, barrel-chested and wide of shoulder, with bandy legs that barely seemed adequate to the task of supporting him. He alit from his litter and rolled toward them, his walk betraying his long career at sea. Murgom squinted toward Qala. She suspected he couldn't make out who she was.

But, of course, he knew whom to expect. "Qala, I greet you," he said, giving her the least of bows. "Or Lady Qala, is it now?"

"Qala is fine," she responded. "Welcome to Melawhem."

"Ah, that is a fine name for an estate! Corad told me of its meaning in his Sharshic tongue." That was 'Seafarer's House,' more or less. He

31

looked across the Chas to that estate and then the separating river. "Do we cross on that barge?"

"You, sir, are welcome to come across with me in my boat. We shall let Lord Corad attend to the rest of your party."

"A most excellent idea!" roared Murgom. "Let us be on our way."

9.

Domi and Ranwif shared upstairs rooms in Qala's manor house. These they now vacated for the use of Lord Vullum and his wife, and moved into Qala's old quarters in one of the outbuildings — the ones Samee and Benaro were not using at the moment. With Domi's aid, Corad got everyone situated somewhere.

Murgom, however, had insisted on sailing his hostess' boat up and down Chas a while before going to his lodging. Fortunately, his eyesight was fine when it came to distant objects and he did not run into anything. And she need only rebuff his advances the one time.

The admiral was now settled down in Qala's front room, the one she used as her office, quaffing ale. He squinted toward the two children playing in the corner. One of the older women who had once served as wet-nurse to Zedos was keeping an eye on them for now. "Neither of them is mine, I would guess," said Murgom. "Xit?"

"So it is. The boy. His playmate belongs to his nurse." When Murgom peered at the stout woman seated in a wooden chair, intent mainly on her knitting, Qala added, "Not her. The girl's mother is away for the nonce."

"Lady Belema hinted something of this," the old sailor told her, and took another quaff of his ale, draining the cup and looking about for the pitcher.

Corad refilled for him. "My parents surely have had their suspicions about the paternity of Zedos," he said. "More so, in light of the name given the boy."

Hurrum and Belema knew the cover story for Qala giving birth, that his father was a man of the south, a trader slain by the pirates. They would not question that publicly but certainly were astute enough to suspect Xido. But it was likely they thought him a sorcerer, not a god. "I am grateful for their discretion," said Qala.

"Part of being neighbors," the nobleman replied. "And keeping up appearances." He turned his attention back to the Muram admiral. "I trust you will make no mention of this to Lord Vullum and his wife, sir."

"I was keeping deeper secrets before you were born, boy." He chuckled amiably. "Mostly from my wife."

Corad nodded. "Good, for I believe I hear them on the stairs."

A maid ushered the pair in a minute later. They were as Qala remembered them a year and more past, at the time of their daughter's wedding to Lord Corad. Vullum, perhaps, had less of the harried look he wore then, but was just as thin. The Lady Galana none could call thin; she was a big woman, though not particularly fat. Tall and full-bodied she was, wide of hip, large of bosom. Handsome of face, too, with features a little too bold for Qala's tastes. Not that she had any designs on the noblewoman.

"Some ale?" she asked, waving them toward chairs. Qala was not inclined to put on airs, no matter how important these two were. "Or I could have wine brought."

"Wine would be —" began Galana and then her mouth fell open as she stared at something in the middle of the room. All heads turned to see a swirling of the air. A moment later, young Damana crouched there, quite naked, though her clothing had also appeared, scattered about on the floor.

"Oh, damn it all!" the girl cried. "Just when I finally got him into my bed!"

The nurse proved the most quick-witted of all there, grabbing up one of the children's blankets while the others gaped, and draping it over Damana's shoulders. The girl pulled it about her and smiled. "So I'm home at last. Budo told me it would happen."

And just in time, thought Qala. Had the girl seduced Budo?

"You run a most interesting household, Lady Qala," observed Vullum. "I think perhaps this young lady could use some privacy."

"Even so," agreed Qala, "and we could use more drink, and a meal too. Let us repair to my hall." To Damana she said, "I shall tell your brother you are back."

She linked her arm with Admiral Murgom's and led all into the central hallway and then left toward the dining hall. The hall and kitchens shared part of a wall with her manor house but were otherwise a separate structure, laid out in traditional Sharshite fashion, a tall central section and lower arcades on either side with arched colonnades, all stuccoed stone. The kitchens lay behind it.

It was built previous to the house, she assumed, although no one who lived on the estate knew anything about it. Before their time. The big manor house would have been thrown up later, as the Damros family who had ruled here grew more prosperous.

Benaro himself came out of the kitchen. "Your sister is back safely," Qala told him. "How fares the rest of the family?"

The cook had kept his composure over the past few days but he looked relieved now, and thankful. "Mother and child are both well, my lady. We've set the naming for day after tomorrow, when the priest of Jov visits." The man made the rounds of estates and villages in the area, including Lord Hurrum's, where stood a small shrine to the chief of Sharshite gods. Qala had met him there the first time she called.

"Well, it seems that Samee may malinger a bit longer now that Damana has returned. Bring us wine, will you, and something to snack on?" He and his helpers would be preparing a full meal later but Qala was hungry now. She assumed her guests would be too.

No need to take the high table she occupied during formal feasts. Qala chose a spot near the kitchen. They could have eaten in the kitchen itself; she frequently did but that might be a tad too informal for these nobles. Cups and pitchers of wine appeared, and pastries of varied sort. Of all the skills Benaro had learned in the kitchens of Lord Hurrum, Qala prized the making of pastry — Muram pastry — most.

Lady Galana and Lord Vullum politely made no mention of Damana, and her sudden and extraordinary appearance. Talk instead turned to the upcoming journey south. "My wife, I tell her, should go no further south. It will be a rough way," said Vullum.

"That it will," agreed Corad. "There are no houses nor inns on that road. I would advise against carrying tents along. Best to travel light and everyone mounted."

Murgom raised a shaggy eyebrow at this. "I'll need my litter, my boy. I've not ridden horseback in decades."

"And if the admiral can travel so, then why can't I?" asked the Lady Galana.

Qala decided to add her thoughts. "The keep of Flawum is hardly worth the visit, my lady. It is old and run-down and cold."

"Indeed," broke in Corad. "You'll find more cheer right here. Why not remain with Qala until we return?"

Qala reined in an urge to kick the nobleman most violently. "Or with Lord Hurrum and Lady Belema," she suggested.

"Perhaps," replied Galana, and gave Qala an appraising look. "Do you hunt, Lady Qala?"

"It is Qala only," she responded. "I am no noble, only a citizen of the empire." Which counted for more than their Sharshite titles, as all were aware. "But no, I have never found the time for the hunt." Nor the interest.

Corad snickered. "Aside from hunting for misplaced humans."

Galana and Vullum glanced at each other. That glance held meanings, Qala knew, but not what they might be. "Such as our daughter," said the nobleman, "and your own son. Sesa has told us much of this."

"Which," took up Galana, "is why we were not too astonished by your maid showing up as she did."

"She was in the world of the gods?" asked Vullum. He took a rather large bite from a scone. "These are exceptionally good. Do you grow the raisins here?"

"They come from upriver," Qala replied. "I've put in vines but they are yet too young to bear grapes. And yes, Damana was in, um, *a* world of the gods."

Galana gave her husband a sidelong look. "Vullum was always rather skeptical of the gods."

"I still am," he declared. "Not of their existence but that they are of any use to us."

Corad leaned back, regarding the nobleman for some moments. "Were it not for certain gods," he stated, keeping his voice even, "neither you nor I might have the Lady Vasema today."

"Then let us hope the gods favor us again," said Murgom.

10.

Despite Corad's advice, many of the men on foot who had accompanied Murgom as far as Melawhem would remain with him on the trip south. Not all, for some were Lady Galana's attendants and guards. Galana had decided to stay on with Qala. Qala was not happy about this.

But she made no complaint. The woman was her friend Corad's mother-in-law, after all, and it was safer. They had all heard more rumor of strange men about. Maybe the noblewoman would tire of the routine of the estate and return soon to Sarowhem. Her entourage was not large enough to be much of a burden. Galana — or her husband — had brought along not a single female servant but there were a dozen men to be quartered and fed. Eight of these were guardsmen, who tended to keep close to their mistress.

"I'll find a maid for you," Qala promised, as the two watched Murgom's expedition assemble by the stables. Galana's litter was to be left behind. Its horses, however, would go along as extras. Two were now being harnessed to the admiral's litter, one before and one after the partially enclosed seat. It was Murgom's own litter, the one he kept at his house in the port city of Azer, down near the Chas's mouth, and appeared practical and simply detailed.

"I don't really need a litter myself, you know," said Galana, not replying to the offer of a maid. "I've been on horseback since I was a small child."

"As your daughter."

"Yes. That is one way she takes after her mother." A laugh, but with just a bit of an edge to it. "About the only way."

Sesa did look like her father. Many rumors circulated about his wife's infidelities but there had obviously been none there. The girl also had his even temperament and was apparently a bit of scholar — if the subject interested her. Galana watched the preparations a little while longer, wordlessly. Then, "Do you think there is danger to them?"

"Corad was attacked when last he traveled south," Qala admitted, choosing to be cautious in her reply.

"As an envoy. Murgom might make an even more attractive target."

Or her husband. "He is well guarded," she offered. Not only by the Muram lancers but by a handful of equesters Corad had brought along.

"Yes," admitted Galana. "I hope no one from my family is mixed up in it. My late brother plotted to restore the Pretender."

Qala knew a good bit about this, probably more than the woman suspected. Corad's sister Marana had been pledged to this brother, Gawif, and had fled with Saj to avoid the marriage. "Some Sharshites surely oppose the treaty," she said. "Some Mura too."

Galana only nodded, so Qala continued. "But the pirates and smugglers who operate in the south might be the most adamant about preventing it."

The woman turned to her. "Oh? No one has mentioned this to me before. Should I speak of them to my husband?"

"Corad is aware of their involvement. He'll take care of it." Not as well as I might, thought Qala. I know those people. But it was not her task; that was up to Murgom and Vullum and Corad. And even Ranwif, who was to accompany them.

At the moment, he was bidding a quite tender farewell to his wife. He had left Domi far too frequently over the past months. They seemed to make up for it when he was home.

Domi sauntered over to the pair now. "Lady Galana," she greeted Qala's guest. "My lady Qala."

"I apologize that your husband will be taken from you again," said the noblewoman.

"It is only a while," Domi replied. "And he will be back before our child is born," she added, breaking into a broad smile. Qala could do no more than embrace the young woman who had become so much a part of her life.

The column was moving now. Vullum mounted and waved a farewell to his wife. He rode rather well, Qala thought, not that she was a great judge of such things. It was time to turn her attention elsewhere. "Domi, you will find a chambermaid for the Lady Galana, will you not? Not Damana. I need her for the children a while longer."

"Certainly, my lady. Do remember that you should attend the naming day for Benaro's son tomorrow. A, um, small gift would be appropriate."

"And you shall choose it. Thank you." Domi recognized this as a dismissal and went off to her many duties.

Qala and Galana strolled back toward the manor house. "We just give a coin on these occasions," remarked Galana.

"As do I for most of my people," Qala replied. "Samee and Benaro are a little more important to me."

The Sharshite woman sniffed. "A good way to arouse jealousy among the peasants."

"Or a reminder to better themselves." They had a different view of the world. Best not to argue it. "Would you care to see the estate?" she asked.

"I would. Honestly. But right now I think a little lunch and a siesta is more in order, don't you?"

Qala had not picked up the Sharshite habit of midday naps but was willing enough to agree. She could catch up on things in her office while Galana slept. It was to be hoped her guest was not one to sit up late. Qala was early to bed most nights.

An hour later, she was at her accounts book. The children and their nurse had retired to the nursery where, Qala suspected, all three napped. It was quiet outside; the peasants here also observed siesta, except when there was a crop to get in. Sometimes even then.

Perhaps she heard something. Perhaps she somehow felt it, but the Muram woman turned to see shadows swirling and coalescing in the corner. It was not unexpected after recent events. Budo stepped out of the darkness.

"You're here to see if the girl arrived safely, I would hazard," said Qala. "It is long since I have seen you, Budo."

The big homely god sheepishly answered, "Sorry, Qala. We lose track of time in our world."

Mawa came out the shadow behind him, and Lenco after her. "It's one of the perils of being immortal," said the latter. "So little Damana made it back in one piece?"

"Without her clothes," replied Qala, looking from one to the other. She would accuse none of them of anything but they should know she had a mind to. "She won't say what she was up to. Or with whom."

She was surprised by the trio's baffled expressions. At last, Budo reluctantly uttered, "Xonxon. It must have been."

"I'll give him a speaking to when we return," promised Mawa.

"It seems they didn't get far enough for it to be a problem," Qala told them. "It also seems that the girl seduced your poor mafadwi."

Budo nodded solemnly. "She tried to get into my bed, too," he admitted. "Still, I shall have some words with the boy. Me, not you," he directed to Mawa. The goddess shrugged.

And Lenco laughed. "Mawa might not have acquiesced to our half-brother's wishes so readily once. Budo has come up in her estimation."

"As well I should," responded Budo the Boar. He was not completely without wit, even if he could never match his siblings.

Mawa and Lenco perched on chairs now; Budo leaned his massive body against the wall. "So, did the girl behave in your world otherwise?" asked Qala.

"Too well," said Budo. "Too trusting. Zedos protected her."

"The mafadwi are a bit in awe of your son. They see the god in him," added Mawa.

Budo nodded. "I took her to my cave as soon as I could. Zedos too. He hadn't been there before."

Qala sighed. "Is he likely to go visiting you now?"

"Entirely likely," came from Lenco. "Mong is drawn here by the presence of Zedos but I believe the boy is as we are —" He swung an arm toward the other two gods. "Able to travel from world to world at will. He only needs be taught how."

"And should be taught, lest he get in trouble," said Mawa.

The other two murmured agreement. "Our friend Flawum probably can do it too," Lenco went on. "And perhaps he shouldn't be taught. The fact that he impregnated three mafadwi demonstrates that he truly was in our world and no longer tethered to this one. I doubt he would ever have been pulled back here."

"We can only guess what gifts the children he left behind might have," spoke Budo. "I shall be the one to keep an eye on them. These two can't pay attention long enough."

"Too true," agreed Lenco. "If only Zedos's father would show

40

himself. He is the most powerful of us all, you know. He could rule our world if he wished."

"What with Krat being gone," said Mawa.

"Maybe even if he wasn't gone. But now we must be gone," Lenco announced, and pulled darkness in around himself. His siblings followed him into shadow.

11.

Galana reminded Qala some of Marana. Both were tall women — though not towering ones — but Galana had more curves to her and lacked some of Marana's width of shoulder. The Sharshite noblewoman was perhaps half a decade older than Qala.

However much that was. Qala was uncertain of her own age. She thought she must be near forty now.

The pair rode about the estate, followed by Babo and Sorg, and two of Galana's own men on borrowed horses. Qala would have preferred to walk.

"That is maize, isn't it?" asked her guest, surveying a field of shoulder-high green. Maize was a relatively new crop in Sharsh, introduced from the south. As far as Qala knew, it was not grown across the sea where she had been born.

"Yes," she said, "we grow much maize here. It is a most useful crop." She was unabashedly proud of being a pioneer in its cultivation.

"Vasema has spoken of it at times," said Galana. "And these are ground nuts. I can recognize them."

"We rotate between the two," Qala told her. "It's better for the soil."

"My daughter would say something of that sort. Are ground nuts good to eat? I've never had one."

"Not bad. They make for good fodder anyway." Many of the peasants enjoyed them boiled. Qala was not so fond of the nuts that way but did like them roasted.

Galana had few questions and those not very discerning. She seemed to have little knowledge of or interest in the everyday running of an estate. Quite unlike her daughter. She only wrinkled her nose at the pig sties, Qala's greatest pride and greatest maker of money.

"And you never hunt," the woman said. "There are forests all around you here."

"We avoid them," replied Qala, "for the most part. It is lawless beyond our fences. Perhaps Murgom's negotiations will change that. But," she continued, turning to look back the way they had come, "the estate does include some land on the other side of Chas. Not nearly as much as south of the river, and never farmed. I may see about cutting the timber over there someday. I do permit my people to take game from the woods."

Galana shook her head. "A bad habit for peasants."

"Not so long as they know they must share their catch with me," said Qala. "A haunch of venison, the extra rabbit they take. That's the rule when they fish the river too. A tithe for the lady of the estate!" She could not help grinning.

"Hmm, as long as there *are* rules."

"Exactly. People must know what is permitted and what is not." So she and the Lady Galana could agree about something. No need to mention that the rules on game were not strictly enforced at all. She trusted her people to behave, most of the time.

"My lady," called out Sorg. "Time it be for baby-naming."

Qala looked up at the sun. Yes, it was near noon. "Do you wish to come?" she asked her companion.

"Why not?" laughed Galana. "I might as well see everything." They rode in the direction of the river for a minute or two before she added, in a more serious voice, "You take great pride in this estate and in your people."

"I do," admitted Qala. "It is a home I never had before." Why would she say such a thing to her? She barely knew the Lady Galana. But the woman had recognized Qala's love for Melawhem, hadn't she?

The ceremony was in a grassy field by the river, the same field that was now used for most celebrations and festivals. Sheep grazed there on other days. Qala need take no part; her presence was enough. She did alight from her steed. It would not do to separate herself from her people in that manner, to sit a horse looking down on them. Galana, after a moment of hesitation, did likewise.

The priest of Jov, his long beard streaked with gray, spoke in Sharshic. Qala could follow it well enough these days. She assumed Galana was fluent, but more and more the Sharshite nobility spoke Muram rather than their native tongue.

Gifting would be later. Domi would make certain something appropriate was delivered. Samee and Benaro stood before the priest, holding the infant. What name might they have chosen? Qala learned soon enough; the priest held the boy up before the small crowd and announced, "Ranwif!" So they had named him for Benaro's best friend and foster brother.

"Do you know the story of Ranwif and the family of Benaro?" she whispered to Galana.

"They took him in when the Damros family was slaughtered, didn't they?"

"So they did. I didn't realize the tale was widely known."

"Vasema gave it to me. You must remember she has become a great friend of your Domi." Galana's dark eyes fixed themselves on Qala. "I would be your great friend, if I might."

Oh, ho. She could take that many ways, and it would be wise to avoid all of them for the moment. "Let's get some lunch," she said. "Sorgo, take our rides to the stables, please."

"Your best cook won't be available," Galana pointed out. The parents were surrounded by a crowd of family and well-wishers. The woman turned her eyes toward Chas. "It is nice to live on a river, I think. You and Lord Hurrum are fortunate."

"I do not think I could live away from the water," Qala responded.

"Vullum's estate lies near the River Indor, but not on it. My own family comes from the hills."

Qala knew that family had vast holdings, even after the Mura had confiscated some of her late brother's estates. They were too powerful to throw down as had been some of the other old families. Families such as Ranwif's.

"I must take you sailing while you are here," she said.

"I would like that," said Galana, almost whispering.

Benaro might have been absent, but his assistants were quite capable of producing a meal. Qala took her single guest into the kitchen to eat this time. "Simple fare it will be," she said, not to apologize but to inform.

"I have eaten many a rough meal when on the hunt," responded the noblewoman. She attacked the bacon and greens and corn cakes set before them with admirable gusto.

She is a woman of appetites, thought Qala. I am surprised she is not much fatter. The priest of Jov wandered in. "Join us," she called to him. Qala knew little of Sharshite religion nor had much desire to learn more, despite having met one of their goddesses.

"Tell me," she said, as the man filled a plate, "are there any priestesses of Esefa about these parts?"

"Esefa is honored at all the shrines of Jov," he responded.

Qala frowned. She hoped it was not too theatrical a frown. "The wife of Jov should have her own shrines. Wouldn't you think so, Lady Galana?"

"Absolutely," said she, between mouthfuls.

"Perhaps I'll build one here. See if you can find me a priestess, will you?"

The man seemed slightly bewildered.

"I," announced Galana, "trained in her temple as a girl. Alas, my duties to my family prevented me from taking up the duties of a priestess."

"The temple in Indabas, my lady?" asked the priest.

"No, a shrine in the hills, on our family's estate." She seemed lost in the memory for a few seconds. "You truly should build one, Qala."

Better than a temple to Orgum or one of the other Muram gods, Qala told herself. She had little faith in the gods of her childhood these days.

There was Damana. Qala had spied her at the naming ceremony. "Ready to go back to minding the children?" she called to the girl.

"Yes, my lady," she replied. "I came to fetch their lunch."

Domi must have already set her to task. "That's good. We'll be along later." She wondered if she should say anything about her escapade in another world. No, it would be to no purpose. But if Damana ever found her way back there she should know the dangers of stealing a mafadwi's mate. It really might eat her!

Galana napped again on their return to the manor house and Qala spent some time in the company of Damana and the two little ones. But they were sleepy too so, in time, she wandered out into the afternoon. It was quite still, only the song of the cicadas breaking through the sultry silence. They were well past the midsummer and but a week from Zedos's birthday.

12.

Someone was at the door. Damana? Could there be a problem with Zedos?

No, she would have rapped, would have spoken. "Who is there?" she asked the darkness.

"Me." Galana. Qala felt the woman sit down on the side of her bed. Then she bounced up and down a couple times and ran her hand along the mattress.

"Whatever is inside this bed?" she asked.

Qala smiled an unseen smile. "Corn husks. I told you it was a useful crop."

Nothing was very fancy in Qala's house, even in those rooms upstairs. The beds had neither curtains nor canopies, but some boasted feather mattresses and pillows. Not Qala's own bed.

"I must test it," declared Galana. There was a rustling; it took a moment for Qala to recognize it as the removal of a robe. Then she slipped beneath the thin sheet. "Not too bad."

"It's good enough for me," whispered Qala. "I have slept more than once directly on straw. Or on dirt, for that matter." She reached out her hand and found Galana.

"Then this is good enough for me," was the whispered answer, as they came together.

The next few days — when Qala's duties as mistress of the estate allowed — were spent much in each other's company. It was company both enjoyed. They rode on horses, and up and down Chas in Qala's boat. Galana became quite passionate about the boat and the river, and about Qala, for that matter.

But Qala recognized that she did not have any great passion of her own to return. It was idyllic, to be sure. The nights were shared as well. Both were skillful in bed. Perhaps both simply longed for someone to love. And both knew it would end, this summer, this love.

"Tomorrow is Zedos's big day," Qala said. She had been mentioning this frequently.

And Samee would return to the nursery, at least some of the time.

That she was nursing the baby was no problem. Damana could stay on and help.

Galana nodded amiably, as she had at the previous announcements. "I'd best go upstairs and clean up for dinner," she said. That would be something simple, brought to Qala's chambers, followed by quiet conversation and playing with the children. Later — ah, later, Qala would steal up the stairs to Galana's room. The woman quite refused to part with her feather bed again.

Qala had the windows open in her own bedchamber, letting in the fragrant warm air of this summer evening. As she poured out a basin of water, the room seemed to shimmer, shards of light forming and reforming until a tall blond woman in a sky blue kyrtle stood before her. She had known it would be Esefa before ever she took shape.

The goddess tilted her head and regarded her. "Galana?"

"You suggested it," Qala reminded her. Nearly two years ago, true.

"So I did," admitted Esefa. "You and I know it is a dalliance. I hope poor Galana recognizes this too, but she seems quite taken with you."

"She will become quite taken with someone else as soon as we part."

Esefa smiled, but there might have been a tinge of sadness to it. "Maybe so. I would like the Lady Galana to know true love but she does seem hopeless, going from one passion to another. Be that as it may, I did promise love to you. I have not forgotten that, Qala."

"I have my son. It is enough."

"So you tell yourself now. So you try to convince yourself."

Qala could find no answer to that. Perhaps the Queen of the Heavens, the goddess of love, was right. So she changed the subject. "I would guess you have been keeping an eye on Flawum, my lady?"

"And his unexpected children? Indeed so, Qala." Esefa stopped in thought a moment. "Not the ones he begot on the mafadwi, not directly. Budo is helping me there. We both worry about them."

As long as they stayed put, Qala saw no need for that. But they might not. Maybe, like Zedos, they would be able to travel from one world to another.

"Flawum himself needs little attention these days," the goddess continued. "He found love, and has healthy and quite normal children in this world."

"Lenco thinks he could be able to travel between worlds."

Esefa slowly nodded. "You know of Jov's father, Gren?"

"Some of my people mix him up with Orgum these days." Qala did not approve of that sort of thing and it was evident in her voice.

"Indeed, very different gods, though neither is the most pleasant of beings." She stated this quite matter-of-factly. "Gren was the greatest of the Ancient Ones, the primordial giants who came before the gods, and ruled over them and his world until he was deposed by his son."

"Your husband."

"Even so. But Gren's brothers and sisters remain an unruly lot. One of Jov's uncles raped or perhaps seduced Flawum's great-grandmother. She seems to have gotten herself involved in the worship of the Ancient Ones." Now it was Esefa who clearly showed her disapproval.

Qala searched through the little she knew of the Sharshite pantheon. Wouldn't Esefa's own parents be numbered among those giants?

Perhaps the goddess suspected her thoughts, for she said, "Much of the truth of our origins is lost in the mists of Chaos. But know that Flawum has the stuff of divinity in him. It may or may not show itself in his descendants." The infinitely deep sapphires of her gaze met Qala's own dark eyes. "As with your son. I have been told of his abilities."

"Perhaps he'll come and visit you someday." Qala spoke it as a jest but knew it might be possible.

"Our world has even more dangers than that of his father," warned Esefa. "But we have gotten quite off the subject, have we not? I still need to find love for you, Qala."

"I thank you for trying, my lady." She laughed at a sudden thought. "And if you succeed I shall most certainly build a shrine for you here."

"Ah, now I have true incentive. Jov and I are forever contesting who will have the more holy places." The goddess smiled as she dissolved into light. "It's part of being in love, you know."

13.

"Have you considered building a tomb for yourself?" asked Galana. "I noticed the Damros sepulchers on our ride this morning."

"I would prefer sky burial, as is the tradition of my people."

Galana seemed taken aback. "I did not know any of you practiced that these days."

"Keep in mind that I am not of Muradon," said Qala. "I was born in the old kingdoms, across the Great Sea."

"It seems almost like the way of the Jevotes, who discard the body as of no more importance."

"We Mura do not deny the value of the material body. That is why we allow it to give one more service to the world." That sounded good, didn't it? Where had she heard it?

"Hmmph. I think I would prefer to feed the worms rather than the vultures."

"We would do neither, shut up in marble tombs." Qala knew her ancestors had been nomads of the steppes. Sky burial had simply been practical for them. She had to admit it held no great meaning for her — admit it to herself, not to Galana!

"You will attend the birthday party," she said. Her tone implied there could be no refusal. "And bring a gift."

"Of course. I've one ready." Was there a sigh? "I hope to be gifting a child of Vasema and Corad one of these days."

"Then Corad should stay home more," declared Qala.

"That's the problem with wedding an important man." Galana seemed ready to leave it at that for a few seconds. "Such as my own husband," she added. Her voice, often strident, had become a throaty whisper. "Vasema is all we have. There is no male heir."

For a moment, the rumors of the noblewoman's affairs flitted through Qala's mind. If they were true, there had been other opportunities for Galana to conceive. Unless those lovers were all like Qala!

"Then, um, would a son of Corad and Sesa inherit Vullum's estate?" He should in Muram law, but Sharshite rules might apply.

"No, it goes to a cousin. But my own holdings should pass to their child."

Which were considerably more than Vullum's, Qala was aware. No point in pondering that until there actually was an heir. "We'll have the party down by the river," she said, returning to their original topic. "A small gathering. It's too fine a day to be indoors."

Galana looked to the sky. "I think it might rain."

Qala had to agree. She could direct Domi to put up a tent, maybe. No, it would simpler to move to the hall, if need be. "We shall see. I suppose you will want your siesta now."

"You could join me," suggested Lady Galana.

It was tempting. "Too much needs doing," she replied, albeit reluc-tantly. "And it would keep you from sleeping."

"Not that I would mind. Very well," Galana said, rising from her seat. "I shall expect a birthday present from you later on." She passed out through the back door of the office, toward the central hallway and stair-case.

Qala settled down at the oval table of dark wood at which she often worked, though she had also a small desk in her bedchamber. She could not concentrate this day. She got up and peeked into the nursery. Zedos and Letta were napping, and so was Damana. Samee rocked in the corner, humming a song to herself, her little one at her breast. She smiled serenely at Qala when she saw her standing there.

No point in going in. She went back and stared at the papers on the table for a minute or two, trying to focus. The door to the outside hung open and she could see it was growing dark. Storms would indeed force them indoors this afternoon. Zedos had been born during just such a storm so perhaps it was appropriate.

Why was she standing here? She strode out into the afternoon, down to the lawn by the river. It was but a week till the Feast of Plenty, when a much larger celebration would take place on the spot. Servants were already removing the tables they had just set up. Domi was a step ahead of her again.

She followed the workers back toward the house. The storm was moving up behind it, out of the south, a towering slate-colored mass of cloud with lighting playing along its belly. We must make sure Letta's birthday is not forgotten amid all the revelry of the Feast of Plenty, she told herself. No matter that the little girl would probably not remember.

A first wave of driving rain hit and she ran on to shelter. Qala did not mind the storm. She might have stood right there and let it pass over her, pour itself into her and she into it, had she not chores to attend. Domi was in the manor hall, directing the servants, conferring with Benaro, scolding those who had dripped on the stone floors.

"I am afraid I am leaving something of a puddle too, Mistress Domi," said Qala.

"So is the roof," replied the young woman, pointing out strategically placed buckets. "We must get up there and find the leaks."

"Later, I would hope. Is all ready for our boy?"

"Half an hour, my lady. Or whenever the little master wakes up."

"I doubt anyone could sleep through this racket," said Qala. Thunder roared behind the rain drums on the roof. "I'll go get ready." She headed toward the double doors that opened into the manor house. Galana had surely been awakened by the racket, though her room was on the north side, away from the wind. Right above Qala's own chambers, in fact. The suite gave an excellent view of River Chas.

But Qala liked being able to readily step outside. She was quite willing to let Domi and Ranwif occupy those rooms. If they departed she did not think she would put the new bailiff up there. The couple were almost family. No, they were family. It was quiet in the common room. She slipped into her own sleeping chamber, which opened off the east end of the room, with the nursery opposite.

Nursery now. It was unlikely that had been its original use. Dry clothes — she should don something better than she usually wore. Better? This was her son, the most important thing in the world to her. She should wear her best, not her better. Qala did have some decent gowns, purchased in Azer before she came upriver to claim her estate. Ah, once she ruled from her dais, Queen of Pirates, wearing a simple kilt and sleeveless blouse, the same as most of her followers. It was the sword at her side and the brain in her head that had mattered, not her clothes. Zedos must learn that lesson.

This one, of blue silk. She slipped it over her head, smoothed it against her slender body. Galana will like this, she couldn't help thinking. Thunder rattled the shutters, closed and latched against the storm. It would be nice to have a glass window or two in this place. No, too frivolous. Better to repair the roof!

A pair of soft leather slippers on her narrow but not so short feet. She crossed the office to the nursery to find all awake and ready. Letta was bright-eyed with excitement; Zedos seemed to be taking things with more reserve.

"Mommy," he said. "Ungle Boo gum?"

"I think not, my dear," she told him. "I am sure he might visit some other day." Silently, she hoped the boy wouldn't take a notion to visit Budo's cave himself. "Why don't you lead the way to the hall?"

The procession was, of necessity, a slow one, for Zedos's legs were short. Yet he led them on, surely, into the manor house's central hallway. He seemed a bit less certain where to turn from there.

"We must see if Lady Galana is ready to join us," she told him. "Wait while I go up and fetch her."

He gave a grave nod. Zedos took his duties as leader seriously. Qala climbed the bare wooden stairs and rapped on her guest's door. "Oh," said Galana, "I am just about ready." She did not appear ready at all, half dressed and her hair unruly. The noblewoman peered past Qala. "Who is this?"

Qala turned. Somewhere in the dim passageway another had joined her, a slight and wiry, very dark man in a simple white tunic. He was rather homely but seemed to possess an air of endless vitality.

She gave him a long look. "This," Qala said, "is Zedos's father."

Part II.
RELATIVELY DIVINE

14.

Zedos's eyes were fixed on this strange visitor. What might the boy suspect? Qala had introduced him to all simply as her old friend Xit. They could sort the rest out later. The birthday party came first and she intended nothing to spoil it.

Domi knew the true story of the father of Zedos and might recognize Xido as such. Some of the others knew some of the facts. Samee, Benaro. Even Damana, who had recently learned somewhat more first hand.

The other guests would have no idea. Some of these were children. Not friends of Zedos, of course; he was still too young to form much in the way of friendships. By next year, that should change, or so Qala had been assured. She did know all children enjoy parties and the food that goes with them.

One friend did appear, however, when Mong popped in — and not alone. Xido was the first to spy him, and beckoned him to join the celebration. It was not surprising that Mong would be shy among so many humans. It was surprising that another was with him.

"So, you have come to join the party, have you?" asked Xido. The little monster nodded. "Mong, isn't it? And this must be your sister."

"Jong," the mafadwi boy announced. She was, for a little girl, exceptionally large. Surprisingly human looking, too, thought Qala.

And able now to come to this world, not 'stuck' anymore. She could not begin to guess why that might be so. Jong plopped down on the floor and regarded them with large dark eyes. As her brother, she was naked.

Oops, not potty trained, either. That would be for Domi to deal with.

"Leave gift!" said Mong, and laughed uproariously. That set off most of the other children there and some of the adults.

Damana came over and moved the little one to a clean spot. "We need cake for this one," she called out. "Why don't you go sit with Zedos?" she asked Mong.

The mafadwi boy need only be asked. Qala very much approved of the girl's poise with these strange little ones. People misjudged her maybe. Oh, she would know Jong already, wouldn't she? From her visit to the cave of Ir. She did not approve so much of the looks Damana was giving Xido.

"Do you think they have they ever eaten cake before?" Galana whispered in her ear.

"I much doubt it," she replied. "Mong *has* nibbled human food on his visits to the nursery. I am not sure what they eat at home." Perhaps it would be best she did not learn.

Mong took a place beside his 'brother,' squirming his way in between Zedos and Letta. Samee stood behind them. "We must sing the birthday song first," she maintained. This was a hoary tune known to every Sharshite. Qala had heard it sung even on pirate ships, despite their mainly Muram crews.

The beginning was ragged. Qala did not attempt to join in. She had no voice and there was no reason to provide proof of it. One strong voice began to lead — the Lady Galana singing the song as it should be sung. The rest followed her.

And whose was that sweet voice wordlessly accompanying her? Qala's was not the only head that turned toward it. Little Jong was standing somewhat unsteadily on her fat legs, singing along in perfect pitch even if she knew not one of the words. Or any words. Xido only glanced at the mafadwi girl and slowly nodded his head before turning back to his plate. The god-man ate as prodigiously as ever he had.

Then cake for all. It was a great slab of a cake, flavored of molasses and the spices of the south, smothered in whipped cream, and a thick and fragrant compote of peaches. Benaro had outdone himself. Jong's portion mostly ended up in pieces on the floor. Mong suspiciously tried some and apparently approved, taking his down in three bites. "Want birthday too!" he declared.

"You can always share Zedos's," Qala assured him. "As brothers should."

Jong started singing the birthday tune again, perfectly, apparently for Mong. Galana took it up, inserting 'Mong' where it had been 'Zedos' before. The little mafadwi beamed so broadly Qala thought his head would split in two.

Xido rose. "I think it is time these two returned to their mother," he said. "Come."

Both mafadwi went to him at once. Taking one in each arm, he passed out through the doors, as if going back into the manor house. Qala — and a few others — knew he would step into another world as soon as he was out of sight.

"Well," said Domi, "I think it is time for the gifts."

It was not until much later, as Zedos was being tucked in for the night, that he asked in a sleepy voice, "Daddy?"

"Yes, dearest," his mother whispered, "that was your daddy."

"Best birfday gift," he said, before falling asleep.

Xido would surely return. When? Who could say? Another three years, perhaps, or tomorrow. Galana and Damana sat in the common room, neither speaking to the other. Samee and both her children had gone. This was not unusual. Many nights, it was only Qala and her son in these quarters, though she liked having someone here in case she had to go out.

Even if it were only upstairs to Galana's room. She ought to move Zedos's bed into her own room, Qala told herself. It was really quite a large space for one woman. "You are staying the night?" she asked Damana. Best to make sure of that.

"Yes, ma'am," the girl replied. "Samee told me I should. If you wish it."

"It would be best. Why don't you go to Zedos's room now?" Damana understood at once her mistress desired privacy. Indeed, she gave Galana and her a bit too knowing of a look.

"I think," said Lady Galana, "she is the only person in the world who has figured out what we are up to."

But some out the world had, too. Never mind that. "Damana seems to have little else than sex on her mind, much of the time," Qala replied. "She was definitely eyeing Zedos's father."

Galana came to the point at once. "Will this change things?"

"There is nothing between Xido and me, no bond other than Zedos."

"That is a pretty important bond."

"True enough," admitted Qala. "It is unlikely I would ever have seen him again were it not for our son." Nor met any of his relatives. How different might all have been, had a god not chosen to give her a child?

Why, she would not even know Galana, most likely. Make the best of what you have, while it lasts, she told herself. It was no good to wait on the chance of love tomorrow. "Let's go upstairs," said Qala.

15.

Preparations would take place all week for the Feast of Plenty. It seemed an odd sort of festival to Qala, this day midway between summer solstice and autumn equinox, celebrated with fire and feasting. Some named it the Feast of First Fruits, for harvesting did begin around the time of its celebration.

Most importantly, it was Jov's own special feast. All the playing about with fire was said to symbolize the chief god's lightning. But, of course, people simply liked to play about with fire. It was true, too, that it was the season of summer storms, bringing their own lightning and thunder, at least in this part of the world.

When the day of feasting was done, her people would settle to the tasks of the harvest, their busiest season of the year. Qala would be as busy as any of them.

Word had not yet come from the south. Murgom's embassy was not likely to have hurried on its road and, too, it would take time for a messenger to return. She began to hope that Vullum would come back soon and take his wife home. Not that she minded Galana's company; indeed, she treasured these days. But there would be work to be done and no time for the woman.

Only time to get on with life.

Even now, she was too busy, before the festival and all that would follow. Galana was out riding alone — well, with a pair of guards — while Qala pored over her account books with Domi. Best to get that out of the way this morning.

"I am surprised that it all balances again," she remarked, as they finished up.

"I can add and subtract, Mistress Qala," replied her bailiff, rather dryly. "Sometimes even correctly."

"Better than me, my girl. That I know." It was good that she and Domi could chaff each other so. That would be lost were another to fill the woman's post. "Now, as to the festival. Be sure it is understood I shall not be named Queen of Plenty this time. That should go to one of the young girls." Her people had surprised Qala by electing her last year.

"Yes, my lady." Domi rose from her chair and stretched. "I'll get onto that now, or as soon as I have some lunch. Should I have something sent over to you?"

"No, I'll go to the kitchen later. Run along now. Oh — Samee," she called out. "Why don't you take the children to get something to eat?"

The young woman appeared at the nursery doorway, Ranwif in her arms, Letta and Zedos flanking her. "Very well, m'lady. Come along," she said, and all followed Domi out the rear door.

They should have gone out into the sun, Qala complained to herself. So she did whenever convenient, rather than staying under roof. She looked out the front door, standing open this warm morning. A stroll to the river before getting back to business — and the Lady Galana — was an attractive idea.

"I thought they would never leave," came a voice from behind her.

A voice she knew well. "You did not come and go in this manner once," she told Xido, turning to him.

He shrugged. "I am not as I was when you knew me before. Then I put all my powers aside and become completely human. Now — now I am rejoined with the god in me."

"Xido is a true shape-shifter," put in Mawa, stepping from shadow. "He can do such things more readily than the rest of us."

Qala looked from the one to the other. "Should I expect more of your family?"

"Lenco and Budo are off plotting something," said Xido.

"Of all of us, Lenco always was the most friendly to Budo. But I," Mawa admitted, "do get along better with him than I used to."

"I suppose even I have warmed to my brother some."

Mawa smirked at him. "You needed a few millennia more of maturity, maybe."

"Maybe so," said Xido.

Qala still stood in the doorway, regarding her unannounced guests. "Are there are no other siblings?" she asked. She had wondered. After all, gods were extraordinarily long lived and had plenty of opportunities to produce offspring. If they chose.

"Oh, to be sure. Neither Krat nor the Old Scorpion were faithful to each other," Mawa said.

"Scorpion?"

Xido's voice was uncharacteristically grave as he answered. "The Scorpion is mother to all four of us."

But only Budo and Xido were fathered by Krat. Someone had mentioned this to her before. Lenco, she was pretty sure.

"It is other siblings who concern us at the moment," spoke Mawa. The goddess was as when Qala had first seen her, her compact body clothed only in a close-fitting silvery kilt about her hips. "Mong and Jong. Jong's appearance here was very much unexpected."

Xido nodded his agreement. "Whether Mong somehow drew her along or she is able to travel among the worlds herself is the question."

"If she can, that brings her close to being a god," said his sister.

"Ir is her mother, no? She is one of the more powerful mafadwi I have known."

Qala knew nothing of that but she was aware of something else. "Remember her father, too," she reminded the pair.

"Yes," said Mawa. "There is a Sharshite god on that side."

"An Ancient. She looks a bit like one of them." Xido pondered a moment. "It is to be seen whether she can learn to separate her natures. If not, she remains a mafadwi, no matter how powerful she might grow."

"Perhaps," was all his sister had to say about that. "But be warned," she said to Qala, "the girl may show up again. If she does it on her own, we will know more."

"And it will become imperative that we undertake her training," added Xido.

"Even so. It wouldn't do to have an unschooled mafadwi bouncing about from world to world."

No, it wouldn't. Qala could see that. "What about my own son?" she asked. "Our son, Xido. Won't he need training as well?"

"That," replied Xido, "goes without saying."

Mawa laughed. "But being talkative gods, we'll say it anyway."

"Hmmph. You and Lenco are talkative, anyway. We will keep watch on the boy, Qala, all of us."

"Even Budo," Mawa slipped in.

"Yes, even Budo. I would have to admit he might be best suited to training Zedos. Or Jong, if need be."

"And now," said Mawa, "your girlfriend is on her way from the stables. We'd best slip away. Unless, of course," she added with a wink, "the Lady Galana might be interested in a threesome."

Xido shook his head. "Let's not muddy up what they have, sister mine. I suspect its ending will be complicated enough as it is."

Mawa sighed. "Xido was ever the wisest of us." The pair stepped back into shadow and disappeared.

16.

Several little streams crossed Qala's estate, flowing north into Chas, either directly or first joining forces. Most were narrow enough to leap — or even step — across. One of the larger flows had been dammed to create a pond for watering the livestock, before continuing to the river a little east of the docks.

These went nameless for the most part, but the largest was called Minnow Creek. This was a marshy affair, almost a slough, that marked the western boundary of Melawhem. Much of the area west of Melawhem tended to wetness, isolating her somewhat in that direction.

Thickets of elderberries grew along Minnow Creek, as well as here and there on the banks of the Chas, and the fruit would ripen shortly. In the spring, they had been thick with bees. I should have more hives, Qala told herself. I'll mention it to Domi.

They should work out the details of who could be spared to pick the berries too. It was work for young people. The elderberry wine and the elderberry-flavored mead, however, were for those a little older! These Sharshites loved their fruited meads.

All that later. The Queen of Plenty was about to be announced. The girl chosen would be aware of it, of course. It would not be sprung on her as it had on Qala. It had been expected that she would then choose a King of Abundance to preside over the feast at her side. Qala had been quite unprepared and named the first man to come to her mind, Ranwif. Looking back, it was not a bad choice — the new owner and the last scion of the family that once held sway here as Queen and King. It was good symbolism.

Domi knew the name of this year's queen too, as she had to plan the ceremonial entrance. It was growing dark and torches were being lit. That was part of the staging. Four of the largest men of the estate now approached, swinging their brands back and forth overhead, supposedly in emulation of Jov's lightning. Fortunately, the god had held back on providing any of the real thing. Behind them came the queen, in a long green gown. Qala recognized the peasant girl but couldn't put a name to her right then. She probably had a boyfriend to name as king.

Samee stood near Qala, keeping an eye on Zedos and her own two children. Her husband had been busy with preparing the feast all the day, coming and going. Damana had been coming and going too, but boys rather than work had been the reason. Now she said, "Next year, that'll be me. Just you see!"

"If you don't get yourself pregnant first," observed her sister-in-law. "You know, this is really an Ildin holiday you Sharshites stole from us."

"I'm not surprised," replied Qala. "Now hush." The queen had been handed a crown of flowers, like to the one on her own head, to give her king. Ah, Dovos. He was a good lad. He kissed his queen well. Erla, that was her name. Or Erlatima, properly. Maybe the two would be standing together before a priest soon.

There was applause as the pair took their dais and then attention turned back to the serious affair of feasting. "Sharshites truly are thieves," came a voice at her elbow. "They had a reputation for it a thou- sand years ago when they were wandering savages."

"Ah, Xid — um, Xit. I did not expect you."

Galana turned away from the peasant pageantry. "Wandering savages?"

"As were all peoples if one goes back far enough, my lady," responded the dark god. "Mistress Samee is right about this festival. It borrows much from those who came before them." He gazed at the revelers. "Not the bit with the torches."

Qala was somewhat surprised that he would openly show himself here. Xido looked entirely presentable too; his siblings had a way of not noting human customs of dress and manner. He really did know much more of mortals then they.

"Daddy." It was more a statement than aught else, and the boy's tone suggested caution more than aught else.

"Yes, that would be me, Zedos."

Qala felt she should speak up at once. "My folk believe his father died before he was born. It would be best if they continued to believe this."

"I'm not sure how many take that tale as the truth anymore, m'lady," spoke Samee. "They've seen too much."

They were seeing things now. More than a few curious eyes were turned toward Xido. "But it will continue to be our story," maintained Qala. "Xit will be a relative, an uncle. We'll say it is, um, the custom of your people for Zedos to address you as father. As his closest living male relative. Yes." That all sounded pretty good to her.

Xido gave her a bow. "Quite plausible and quickly spun. I can see it was not only your sword that made you a true queen."

Galana shook her head. "A queen? I find I know less and less about you, Qala."

I should tell her the whole story, Qala decided. Tonight. Maybe the tale of her daughter's adventures in the south lands, too. All that might take two nights.

How many more nights would they have? Ah, no use thinking on that. "Your daddy is going to teach you, Zedos," she said. "But not now. It is bedtime for you. And poor Letta is falling asleep on the grass. Damana! Let's gather up all these young ones and give Samee some time with your brother."

The girl did not appear particularly happy about this idea but did as her mistress asked. Qala had to laugh. "You'll have plenty of other nights to go bothering boys," she told her.

Lady Galana gave another glance toward the noisy and increasingly inebriated gathering and decided, "I shall go with you,"

"And I," said Xido. "Perhaps my boy and I can become better acquainted."

Qala did not feel like letting him get away with this, god or no god. "Your boy? When did you ever have anything to do with him since his conception?" She scowled a bit, for dramatic effect. "And don't give me your story about swimming the oceans. I know you've not been a croco-dile for a good year and a half."

Both Galana and Damana turned inquisitive eyes their direction. The crocodile thing was new to them.

"But I was other things." He picked up Zedos. "Let's get these chil-dren to their beds." They were at the doors of her quarters before he explained further. "I had much to sort out and understand, about the time I spent as a mindless animal. And as a man."

They paused in the middle of the room. "And, of course, it is easy to lose track of time in my home."

"So I have heard from your siblings. Take the children into the nursery, Damana. I — mmm, we will be in shortly." She turned to Galana. "Some wine?"

The noblewoman slowly shook her head. "I think not. You two seem to have much to discuss so I'll be off to my room and leave you at it. But," she went on, "I'll expect you later."

"I assume the Lady Galana meant you," said Xido after she departed.

"Don't get any ideas otherwise," Qala warned. "You know I'm good with a knife." She poured out a couple goblets of tawny wine, handing one to Xido. "Let us lounge Muram-fashion," she said.

Her people, especially those across the sea, were not great users of chairs but preferred cushions on the floor. Qala had made certain this suite had such to accommodate her, though conventional Sharshite furniture was found everywhere else on the estate.

"It is the way of your home too, is it not?" she asked, as both reclined. "I remember no chairs nor tables in the house of Mawa." Nor Budo's cave, for that matter.

"We tend to live simply, in our own world. Too simply, too peacefully. Time can pass unnoticed. This is why I do not stay there so much." He sipped the wine. "But I needed to for a little while."

"Why did you choose to give me Zedos? I know this is something over which you have control." So his siblings had informed her and so had she wondered since.

"Ah, that is not necessarily as it was. Yes, I can choose this when I am fully a god — as I am now. But I put my godhood aside and became human for a time. Or as human as is possible for me. I was like any other man then when it came to such things." He stared into his cup a moment, gently rocking it back and forth before quaffing the last of the wine. "I was willing to trust to luck so it came to the same thing, didn't it? I did choose, in a way, and do not regret it."

"You chose to be a man, with all that might come of it."

"Exactly. I have done this from time to time to remind myself of the ways of mortals. My old friend Banat told me it would be a good idea to do so again. He probably saw something of what would happen."

"Banat? Isn't that an Ildin god?"

"He is. Let's go see the youngsters before they fall asleep."

17.

Damana seemed exceptionally pleased with herself in the morning. When Qala spied the rumpled bed in her own room, she guessed why. "Did you have a boy in here last night?" Qala was more amused than angry. It was a festival night. Things happen.

"No, my lady. No."

Now she did feel herself growing a bit angry. The girl should admit to it. "Don't lie. I can see the evidence in my own bed."

"It wasn't a boy, honest! It was —" Damana gulped. "It was Xit."

For a moment, Qala stared and then could not keep herself from bursting into laughter. "I'll not ask who seduced whom," she said. "Is he still about?"

The girl shook her head vigorously. "No, my lady. He was gone when I woke."

Just as well. The god would pop back in again sometime. "You are much too young for him," she told Damana. She would not tell this young woman her lover was thousands upon thousands of years her senior.

As he had been hers. Ah, there was Samee, come with breakfast for the children, and with little Ranwif at her breast. She must have collected the infant last night, after Qala ascended to Galana's room. "I met Master Xit in the kitchens," she announced.

So that was where he disappeared to. Not another world! "I shall go there for some breakfast myself," she informed the women. "Please inform the Lady Galana if she comes down." Without further word, Qala hurried out the front door and into the early morning. It was foggy yet, with the mists that rose from river and slough. There was the smell of smoke in it, too, perhaps from the smoldering remains of last night's bonfires.

You forgot to slip on shoes, she told herself. Her bare feet were quite wet from the dew. No matter. Her people were used to seeing her so. A few of those people were huddled about tables in her hall but there was no sign of the Baxac god. Maybe in the kitchens.

Yes, there gossiping with Benaro at the cook's own table. Qala slid onto the bench beside him. "Bring me something light," she said. "I overdid yesterday."

As Benaro rose to do her bidding, she turned to Xido. "Damana? Really?"

The god sighed. She was not at all sure it was a sincere sigh. "It happened — and maybe I should have expected it. I hadn't been with a female since last I was with you. Hmm —" Xido's brow furrowed. "Unless it was with another crocodile while in that form. No, no. That couldn't be. All the crocodiles of this world are much too small. I would have been more likely to eat them." With that, having no crocodiles handy, he took a large mouthful of his corn porridge. It was quite yellow. He must have stirred an egg or two into it, the way she liked it herself.

"I assume you did not impregnate her."

A serving girl brought a cup of tea, the tea Qala had transported up Chas from Azer for her own use. It was an addiction from of old, picked up in the tropical south. These Sharshites did not drink tea but she had made sure they understood its brewing.

Xido waited for the servant to leave before offering an answer. "I did not. It wasn't her time anyway."

Qala shrugged. "No harm done then, I suppose." As long as it didn't happen again. "I told Galana about you last night. And about my own past." She laughed. "Enough to get a former pirate hung, maybe!"

"I think the Lady Galana will be discreet. She takes her honor as a Sharshite noblewoman seriously."

"I suppose she does." It wasn't something Qala was likely to think of. "Ah, thank you." The maid had returned with a plate of freshly baked pastries. Just the thing for this morning. "She is very dark for a Sharshite, isn't she?" she remarked, nibbling at one.

"Northern blood, no doubt," commented Xido.

"You mean my people?" Galana did not seem at all Muram to her.

"No, those who dwelt in this land before Mura or Sharshite, or even Ildin. You'll find more of their blood across the mountains."

"I shall take your word for this, as I have no other choice."

"As wise as ever, my lady. It must be admitted Galana spends a great deal of time out in the sun too. But right now she is inside and headed our direction."

Indeed she was. The lady's eyes remained fixed on Xido as she approached. "You do not look much like a crocodile," she commented, taking her seat beside Qala.

"Yet it is who I am. I was and will be the leviathan that swims the seas of many worlds. This does not change."

"Qala has interesting friends. An interesting past, too." She gave her hostess a sidelong look. "She has promised to tell me the tale of the rescue of Zedos tonight."

"That is a tale I would like to hear myself. I do not put complete faith in the versions my siblings have given me." A dry chuckle. "In part, because they not do quite agree on the details."

"My daughter has given me the story too," said Galana, "as she saw it. Pastries? Hmm, I think not. Benaro!" she called, "Bring me something filling, will you? Eggs. I want eggs." She had taken to treating the cook like an old friend since settling in at Melawhem. Galana turned back to her breakfast companions. "I do not think I will invite you up to my room to hear Qala's version, Lord Xido."

"Call him Xit." Qala's raspy whisper did not conceal her amusement. "He's not overly conceited, as gods go."

"Like these siblings he has mentioned. Ah! What have we here?" The serving maid had place a large mug before her. Galana sniffed at it. "Cider?"

"Perry. Pear trees grow well here. Yes, Xit's brothers and sister, and also the Lady Esefa."

The noblewoman almost dropped her drink in astonishment. Foreign gods were apparently one thing but to meet one of her own Sharshite pantheon was quite another matter. "The goddess? You have met the goddess?"

"We have spoken on occasion." Far more than one occasion. And there was no need to mention Esefa's suggestions concerning Galana.

"I was told of this," spoke Xido. "It is another thing of which I would like to hear more."

"Very well. After siesta. I must be busy walking the estate this morning, preparing for the days of harvest to come."

"I shall walk with you, if you permit," said the dark deity. "I would like to see what you have done here."

Galana shook her head. "Not me. I'll amuse myself this morn but you must promise to ride with me on the morrow."

"So I promise." Qala and Xido rose, leaving the Lady Galana to her breakfast. Benaro had set a platter of fried eggs and lean bacon, with many fried cakes, before her. Qala did not doubt she could finish them all off.

18.

Sharshite noblewomen were expected to ride sidesaddle. Galana, as her daughter, chose not to. Both rode exceptionally well. Qala had never considered anything other than straddling her steed. That was the Muram way, regardless of gender.

This morning they rode westward, Augun and one of the Sharshites accompanying them. The guards followed at a discreet distance, far enough back the women would not need to guard their words. There were many words, many things of which to speak, though the two had talked half the night before.

"Too marshy to ride further this way," announced Qala. "North to the river?" That would be the shortest route and she could get back to work, with hours of morning left. Galana was not inclined to cooperate.

"South," she decided. "I haven't seen that corner of your lands."

"Not much there." It was scrub-covered and wet, used mostly for the grazing of cattle. But she turned her horse to the left anyway, paralleling Minnow Creek. They would not ride all the way to her southern boundary, of course.

Not that it was clearly marked nor that anyone had a clear claim on the land beyond it. That was empty of all but the shacks of squatters, generally well-hidden from the eyes of the Muram soldiers who patrolled the roads through the wilderness. All that could change if — no, make that when — Flawum's treaty was signed.

Qala had already warned her agent in Indabas to be prepared to buy up some of that land for her. Within reason; the former pirate still had funds but much of her wealth was tied up in Melawhem. She would not allow herself to go into debt as Lord Hurrum had.

Lady Galana leaned sideways from her saddle, perusing the ground. "Deer," she announced. "Plenty of deer. And dogs or wolves, maybe."

"Or coyotes," Qala said. "I've seen no wolves here."

They entered a stand of pines, planted by someone before ever Qala took possession of the estate. By their size, that could well have been while the Damros family still held it. Big enough to harvest. She would speak to Domi of it.

Their path was no more than a narrow trail, used more by animals than men, and dappled with the green-gold sunlight finding its way through the pine boughs. "Ho, who's that?" called out Augun. The women turned to see a pair of riders coming from behind. No one Qala recognized. She put a hand to the hilt of her knife and wished she had her sword.

That curved blade hung over the fireplace in her own bedroom. But Augun had a sword and was pulling it from its scabbard. His fellow guard turned his steed suddenly, crashing it into Augun's horse, making it stagger. Before the Mur could recover control and balance, he was shoved from the saddle and fell flat on his back.

All the wind taken out of him, thought Qala, and that Sharshite is a traitor. Her knife was in her hand now, as her horse danced nervously beneath her. With her feet on the ground and a sword in her hand, Qala could face any man. Here, the odds were not good. "Run for it," she hissed at Galana. It was surely the noblewoman they were after. Qala was nobody.

Augun attempted to regain his feet. His horse had bolted and was nowhere to be spied. The two strangers spurred their steeds past him, paying the man no attention, heading straight toward the women. Damn it, Galana, why aren't you riding away?

The Sharshite noblewoman suddenly wheeled her horse about and put the spurs to it. Too late, feared Qala, too long frozen. That sort of thing got fighting men killed. She rode toward the intruders, her knife in her hand, and totally uncertain of what she would do. She would decide when they came together!

One reined his steed abruptly, turning it sideways to her, blocking her, as the other slipped by. Where was the treasonous Sharshite guard? Qala slashed with her long knife but it only glided along the man's torso. There was armor under his cloaked form.

And a sword in his hand, a short heavy blade of the old Sharshite infantry pattern. Easy to conceal if need be. He took one swing at her, a swing easily eluded, and then spurred on toward Galana. She wheeled her own ride around to see the Sharshite guard had already slipped ahead of the others and had the noblewoman's reins in his hands. The other two would be with him in seconds.

70

"Augun!" she cried out. "Your sword!" The man had run forward to stand aside her. He handed the blade up without hesitation and she urged her horse forward. Galana had not escaped. The three had her now and had already managed to bind her hands. One began to lead her away as the other two turned back to block Qala's pursuit.

Ah, but the noblewoman was not so easily kidnapped. She slid out of her saddle and onto the ground, taking the fall on her shoulder and rolling as any practiced horseman might. Then she was up and running, pulling at the bonds on her wrists with her teeth.

It was not enough. Her captor rode her down, scooped her up. Qala was then too busy with her pair of opponents to note more. They knew fighting from horseback, knew it better than Qala. They hemmed her in on either side, pinning her steed between theirs, disarming her. "Word will be sent," one rasped, striking her with the flat of his short heavy sword, knocking her out of her saddle. All four rode away, kidnappers and kidnapped, toward the south.

At least they did not take her horse. It had stopped to graze nearby as if nothing at all had happened. Augun caught up with her. "Do we go after them?" he panted.

She only shook her head. There was no chance of catching up. And what could she do if she did? Qala gazed down the trail. They had disappeared. "We must send word," she said. "To Lady Galana's husband and to Lord Hurrum."

Augun picked up his sword where it had fallen on the ground. "I recognized one of 'em, Qala. He used to sail with us."

Pirates, then. That did not tell who they served. Any man could be hired for the right price, pirate or no. "Bring the horse, will you?" she asked. "It's a long walk home."

19.

"You know already we gods are somewhat limited in what we can do in your world," said Xido. "I doubt I would be able to spy out where Galana has been taken. Our friend Saj might. He has both the talent and the tools for the job. I could go ask him to look for her."

"You mean use the Eyes of the Wind."

"He does have the jewels still." His brow furrowed for a moment, as if some forgotten memory had just returned. "In fact, I believe he used them to call me back from my wanderings."

"If you think it can help," Qala replied. She had her doubts. Messengers had been sent to Sarowhem, and south to the court of Flawum. There was no more she could do, and she was sore and bruised and not inclined to exert herself again this day.

The god slowly nodded. "I'll slip away later, back to my own world, and then see about visiting Lorj. Going directly from here is unnecessarily complicated. And tiring."

Qala had heard similar comments from the god's siblings. Something about being tied to their power or other forms or something like that, back in their home. "Then let's have some supper. Here in my rooms, with Zedos." Said Zedos was playing by himself, Samee and her children having already departed for the night.

"Damana," she spoke, "go tell your brother to send us something to eat, will you? And you need not return."

The girl turned from the open window, from listlessly staring out into the dusk. She shot a look at Xido. "Yes, ma'am." Out she went, the long way across the lawns.

"I think she is suspicious of our intentions," drawled the deity.

"Good," was Qala's only comment on that. Let Damana think what she might, even were her suspicions entirely groundless. She and Xido would never be lovers again. "I should have had her light the lamps before sending her off."

"Allow me," offered Xido. He reached out to — somewhere to find a taper and proceeded to light each of the oil lamps. The bright eyes of Zedos followed all this with great interest.

"Me too," said the boy, stretching out his hand. A howl of pain. He drew it back, his fingers singed. Indeed, smoking.

At once, his father had a handful of snow and applied it to the hurt hand. "I see I shall have to begin your training sooner than anticipated," he told his son. The son paid no attention; he was in his mother's arms now, the tears being brushed away.

"No damage," she decided, examining the fingers. "Where did he reach out to?" Qala understood the mechanics of what had happened. She'd seen it done more than a few times.

"Impossible to say. Maybe just my own world." He pondered the little one for a moment. "Zedos may not yet have discovered any others."

But he will, thought Qala. A knock at the rear door and one of the assistant cooks entered, bearing a steaming platter. "Leave it on the table," she said, waving her free arm in that direction.

They did not eat at the table, however, once he left. Qala again chose her cushions on the floor. Should not Zedos learn how Mura lived? It was more than likely he would have to deal with important men and women of the empire someday. Ha, all that conflicted with her intentions to make a Sharshite noble of him, didn't it?

Zedos could sort it out when he was older. Of that Qala was certain. Harder maybe to sort out his other heritage, that of his father. Here he sat with them, looking like a rather ordinary Baxac man. A somewhat homely one — Lenco and Mawa's side of the family definitely fared better in looks than Xido and Budo. "You must first learn how to look into other worlds," he was telling their son, "before trying to bring things back."

The boy would remember nothing of this, to be sure. He was only two. It couldn't hurt, though. "Can you see my world?" he asked. "Try to look into the cave of Ir. You know where that is."

The boy squinted in concentration. "Mong!" He held out his hand. A moment later the little Mafadwi appeared, holding onto it.

Mong was not happy about this. "Go home!" he bleated. "Wanna go home."

"Of course," said Xido. "Perhaps this would be a good time for me, too." He rose and took little Mong's hand. The mafadwi looked very sleepy. "I bid you my farewell for now, Qala. And you, my son." With that he pulled shadow about the two of them and disappeared.

"I think maybe you shouldn't bring Mong here without asking him," said Qala. "It's not at all good manners."

"Alright, Mommy," responded Zedos and helped himself to more mashed yams.

Xido did not expect that, she thought. Nor, obviously, did Mong. The mafadwi might have been napping and jarred awake to find himself here. That would upset anyone, mortal or monster.

"Mistress Qala," came a voice from the front door, hanging open to the evening.

"Come in, Sorg. What is it?"

The bandy-legged ex-pirate shuffled in and gave a respectful nod. "Messenger, ma'am. Come up from Sarowhem, he did." He gestured for the man to come in, a young fellow in drab kilt and blouse.

Qala knew the man. His duties had brought him here before. "What message?" she asked, gingerly rising to face him. How her midsection ached!

"Lord Hurrum is on his way, my lady. Um, that is he will be on his way at dawn tomorrow."

"With armed men, I assume." Not that they would be of any use.

"Yes, ma'am, I think so. A few. It is to speak with you he comes."

"Then we shall expect him." Probably before noon. "Anything more? No? Feel free to visit the kitchen then. Hmm, a little late to go back across the river. Sorg can find you a bed."

Both men recognized this as a dismissal, bowed and slipped out. "It's time to find you a bed too, my son," she told Zedos, lifting him into her arms. "Why don't you sleep in my room tonight?"

She had no one else with whom to share the night.

20.

Not only Hurrum and a handful of equesters rode in on the morrow, but the Lady Vasema as well, with a pair of hounds trotting along by her horse. It was unexpected but not surprising; the lady would be concerned about her mother.

She was also as headstrong as her mother and not one to be left out of things. They met in the inn, rather than crossing Chas, and there Qala gave them all her story. Those parts Hurrum needed to hear.

"So," he spoke, after thoughtfully sipping the raisiny golden wine Nat had brought them, "they said they will make contact." He considered his hostess a moment or two. "With you?"

Qala was not sure. "They could have meant Vullum," she admitted. "Or even you."

Hurrum but nodded. "And her guard was a traitor. A spy. Hmm." He hesitated a moment. "You don't think this man of yours was in on it, do you?"

"Not Augun," interjected Vasema. "He worships his mistress." Qala was not quite so sure of this, but had no reason to distrust the former pirate.

"I do not think he would have told me he recognized one of the kidnappers were he with them," she said.

"Unless he lied to throw suspicion elsewhere."

That was certainly possible. But unlikely, wasn't it? Augun hadn't the brains for it. There was no point in pursuing that question further. "Will you stay and await word?" she asked Hurrum. "Or go after them?"

He leaned back in his chair, looked out toward the river. "No point in pursuit. I knew that before we came. And I do suspect they will contact Vullum or Murgom rather than one of us."

"Unless they prefer to do so indirectly," said Qala. "But we know their intent, don't we? To disrupt the negotiations with Flawum."

"Most likely," he admitted, and drained his goblet. "I shall ride back at once. There is naught to do here and much to do at Sarowhem."

"Which I and the bailiff handle quite well without you, o father of my husband," laughed Vasema. "But you are right, I think. I shall stay here in case word is sent."

"Oh?" The Sharshite nobleman considered this for but a second. "A good idea, Sesa. Now I won't feel guilty about leaving!" He rose, a tall man whose balding head seemed perilously close to the ceiling beams. "I'll be off at once. Shall I leave an equester or two?" Hurrum did not await an answer. "Yes, of course. So you can send one back with any message. Lady Qala." He gave them the suggestion of a bow and strode out to his waiting men.

"Domi will be glad of a visit," said Qala. "Even under such circumstances."

Vasema nodded somewhat absentmindedly. She is not one to show her concerns, Qala told herself, but she is distressed. The young noblewoman seemed composed, occasionally reaching down to pat one of the dogs that lolled at her feet. Her chestnut hair, long and wavy, was pulled back into a ponytail; her rather large nose jutted from an oval face. Sesa was no beauty but she had a vibrancy to her. Her husband-to-be, Corad, had seen this before ever he knew who she was.

Qala felt she was just the sort the nobleman had needed to give him proper direction. Her practicality was already transforming Sarowhem. She eyed the hounds. "I've never kept dogs," she admitted. "There are some about the estate, of course."

"They'll be no bother. Ah, there goes Hurrum." The thegn and his men clattered off downriver. She turned back to Qala. "I remember you had no dogs, but there were cats."

"Cats are useful on a farm," sniffed Qala. "On a ship too." She saw little use for dogs. "Let's get on over to the house." Vasema followed her outside where, indeed, Hurrum had left a pair of equesters and their mounts.

"Stable those here," she told them. "Nat can show you where. Come on across the river later and we'll find you quarters. I suppose you'll want your horse on the other side, Sesa."

"It would be convenient."

"I don't much like the idea of you riding about after what happened to your mother. Or what happened to you when you were here before."

Vasema led her horse onto the ferry barge, following Qala. The dogs seemed hesitant but a firm word from their mistress brought them aboard. "I wish I could get Zedos to obey like that," remarked the Muram woman.

"Two-year-olds are much like cats," stated Vasema. "Curious about everything and impossible to make follow orders."

"You obviously have experience with them. Maybe I'll let you take charge of the boy."

"I thank you no, my Lady Qala." She gazed toward the far bank. "I heard tales of you and my mother. You should know it bothers me not at all."

"But best to mention it to no others," added Qala.

"Indeed. I know my mother and — I think I know you. Neither would harm my father."

No, they wouldn't. The Lady Galana cared for her husband, in her way.

Domi awaited them on the docks. She had known of the meeting but not what would come of it, for what she should be prepared. "Sesa will be staying with us a while," Qala called to her. "You'll have to find her a bed. Unless she prefers to sleep with her horse." Both laughed at the jibe, knowing the Lady Vasema well. Indeed, she might prefer the stables.

"She can share my rooms with Ranwif gone," said Domi, catching the line thrown her and helping to pull the barge up to the dock. "It will be like the old days."

"But not the same rooms." Sesa led her horse onto land.

"Not now. Samee and Benaro are moving back in there. We would be upstairs —" In the rooms her mother had used. Vasema would not have known the reason for the sudden hesitation.

"Space goes unused in my suite," Qala said. "Why don't you stay with me?"

Sesa smirked. "My pups too?"

Well, she had offered and would not take it back. "The dogs too." They weren't all that big.

"Let's get you to the stables," said Domi. "And then something to eat. Oh, what lovely doggies you are." They vied to nuzzle her hand.

Qala waved them away. "Go ahead. I'll be in my quarters." They would be along in time. She could get some things done. The children had already lunched and were napping when she arrived. Samee was half-asleep herself but intent on her knitting.

I should be out in the fields, she told herself. There's much to be done, even if my muscles are still stiff. Let others concern themselves with intrigue and kidnappings. But she had allowed herself to get involved. Pulled Xido into it too.

Some time passed before the young women showed, chatting about something or another. "I am telling this girl she shouldn't have to go upstairs when she is pregnant," said Vasema. "Oh, isn't it wonderful? I just found out!"

If she still lived here when the baby came. Qala had her doubts of this. "We can work something out, I am sure. Ah, Samee, we are going to have a guest for a few days."

The nurse stood in the doorway to the nursery, drawn by the chatter perhaps. "A welcome to you, Lady Vasema." It was a rather stiff greeting. Samee might remember certain unkind — though not really malicious — comments she had made about the noblewoman before she knew her identity. Or she might just remember her station. She was a servant, after all, and not close to either of these women.

Then she saw the dogs. At once she was on her knees and caressing the beasts. "What good dogs you are!"

"Doggy?" Little Letta peered around her mother and broke into a wide smile.

"Is it safe for her to pet them, m'lady?" asked Samee.

"Completely. These are my companions, not hunters nor guards. They love everyone."

It took little time for the girl to make friends, hugging both and being rewarded with much licking. These country people and their dogs! But it would be well if Zedos learned of such ways too. He had joined them but was holding back, looking things over.

Then he seemed to make a decision and disappeared. Vasema gasped; the other women were almost used to that sort of thing. "Where is he?" asked the young noble.

"Off visiting a friend, most likely," Qala told her. "I do wish he would ask first." Of a sudden, the little boy reappeared, holding hands with Mong and Jong. Mong took one look at the dogs, howled in fear and popped back to his own world.

Jong laughed, perhaps at her brother, perhaps at the dogs, and waddled right over to join Letta in fondling them. Zedos, a tad more cautiously, joined them.

"I can see," commented Vasema, "things have changed since I lived at Melawhem."

"And we shall be glad to tell you all about them."

21.

"Both my parents compose rather bad poetry. I am surprised Mother did not share any of it with you."

"I know nothing of Sharshite poetry," admitted Qala. "I heard the epic poems of my own people as a child." And after that, little beyond the songs of ship and tavern.

"Didn't your father make a gift of his books to Lord Hurrum?" asked Domi. "And more than just poetry too, right?"

"Oh yes. Daddy churns out scholarly works, all quite dry and boring. I am afraid maybe his poetry is also."

All three knew it most unlikely that Hurrum had ever unrolled one of those scrolls. Maybe Corad would have or even the Lady Belema, the thegn's wife. "Mother's work, on the other hand, is somewhat lurid."

"It would be nice if a bard stopped here once in a while," felt Domi.

"There are sailors' songs I can give you," offered Qala. "I suspect they would make even the Lady Galana blush."

Domi nodded knowingly. "I've heard Augun bellowing some of them."

"I can bellow every bit as well as he." Domi politely made no comment on that though the girl surely knew the truth of it.

It was slipping into evening. Jong remained, alternating between playing contentedly with Letta and Zedos, or lying down with Vasema's hounds. "Don't you think you should take Jong home?" Qala asked her son. "But don't stay there!" she quickly added.

"Her mother may be worried," Samee put in. She had avoided taking part in the conversation this afternoon, but sat aside, tending to the children when need be, knitting, nursing her own infant son. She giggled then. "Especially if her brother went home with tales of terrifying monsters."

Qala was surprised by Zedos's laughter at the jest. That was something new from the boy. How much he changed from day to day! "Fraidy-cat Mong," he said, and turned to the little mafadwi. "Go home?"

To the surprise of all — including, apparently, Zedos — the girl simply nodded her head and disappeared. "Well, that is something to report to Xit," commented Qala. "Shall we all go to the hall or do we eat here?"

"I'm for seeing the kitchens," spoke Vasema, and then winked at Samee. "You know your husband flirted with me quite a bit before meeting you."

Domi nodded. "It's true. Why if she and Lord Corad hadn't hit it off, Sesa might have your job now." She was finding it difficult to say this as seriously as she intended.

Qala was more than dubious. "Benaro flirted with everyone, Domi, you included." And Vasema would have been more likely to poach her future husband, not Samee's. "But very well, we'll dine in the hall. Come with us, Samee, and bring the children. You needn't come back after. Sesa seems to think she can perform your duties."

"Yes, m'lady." She gathered the trio quickly, Ranwif in her arms.

"We'll get there more quickly if we each carry one," said Domi, scooping up the little girl. Vasema shrugged and gingerly lifted Qala's son.

"Come," she called to her dogs, and they proceeded out the front door and into the dusk.

Someone running toward them, one of the young men who assisted Qala's 'crew' in patrolling the estate. "My lady!" he called out. "A boat pulling in at the dock."

"Traders? Tell them to go across the river to the inn. It's too late for business."

He halted before her, panting lightly. "I think not. They are travelers and they asked for you and for one they named Xido. I — I think they mean Master Xit."

Yes, they did. Who might know he had been here? Who might know him at all? "Very well. Have them tie up and come to me in the hall. I'll not put off my supper for them, nor inconvenience my guest." She nodded in Vasema's direction.

"Yes, my lady." He gave her a salute of sorts and hurried back toward Chas.

A few tables were occupied in the hall. Those who ate there rather than in their own cottages tended to come and go at all hours, as duty permitted. It was rare that a large group sat down to dinner together. Qala led the way to her favored spot, a table near the kitchen doors.

Benaro himself came out, and leaned down to kiss his wife before turning his attention to his employer, the mistress of the estate. Qala quite approved of this. First things first. "Anything left?" she asked.

"Enough, my lady," he replied, "and I'm always ready to cook more if you wish."

"No need. Just bring us what you have. And sit with us, won't you? Your assistants can clean up without your supervision."

He nodded an acknowledgment and reentered his domain. Qala sniffed at the aromas that had wafted out of it and wished he had left the doors open.

They reopened shortly, as the chief cook and two servers brought trays and platters and pitchers to the table. Benaro himself sat down beside his wife and took Letta into his lap. "It is a pleasure to see you again, my Lady Vasema."

"So formal," scolded Domi. "You used to call her Sesa."

"Ah, but I worked in her father-in-law's kitchens for a year and learned the proper deference to a noblewoman." As well as how to speak courteously and without his rustic accent of old.

Vasema snickered. "But he's still a rude country boy at heart, you know."

"We would have him no other way," said Qala.

"So call me Sesa when we sit together as friends, as we ever did. You as well, Samee. Now what have we?"

A bit of everything, it seemed, chicken and ham, freshly baked corn cakes. None of the bread baked each day before dawn. Either gone or Benaro felt it too stale to set before them. Was that lamb stew? And new-picked green beans. Qala must have some of those. "My lady," breathed Domi, nodding her head toward the entry. "Your visitors."

"So they are." She watched the group approach, accompanied by the same young fellow to whom she had spoken. Two women, four men behind them. Fighting men, she would guess, though they wore only knives. Ildin, she would also guess, as was one of the two red-gowned women.

82

The other looked very different. Their leader was quite dark and carried a long black staff. "Lady Qala," she said in greeting, "I am the Cana Lura."

The Sorceress of the Mountains. Marana and Saj had told her of the woman, and their time with her. Qala felt it best to rise to greet her guest. "I welcome you to Melawhem, my lady. Will you join us?"

22.

It was necessary that Benaro cook more after all. A meal was set before the four men at another table; the Cana and her companion sat with Qala's party.

"This is Ramapee," said Lura. "A priestess of Kamat." She was a somewhat young woman, though mature and not particularly noteworthy in any way. Not so with the Cana.

She wasn't Baxac, was she? That had been Qala's first thought. Dark enough to be of that people but with a shock of curling straw-colored hair, this Lura looked to be a woman making a graceful transition from middle-age. Fifty maybe, or a little older, by appearance. If the tales had it right, she was far, far older.

"You came seeking Xido?" she asked. There was no reason not to get right at it.

"Not really. I had only sensed that he was here." She looked across the table at Zedos, seated next to Letta and her mother. "And in a way he still is. Your son, my Lady Qala?"

"He is." She knew also that this woman had been Xido's lover. He had never given her a child. "So what does bring you?"

"I and my people are leaving our home in the mountains. I wished to spread word of this among the Ildin of the south, should any wish to join us."

"Then you will journey southward from here."

"If you permit me to cross your lands, my lady."

"Oh, of course. And you may rest here as long as you wish. I do expect Xido to, um, pop back in again."

The Cana raised an eyebrow at that. "So he has reclaimed his powers?"

"It is so." She noted that the woman did not touch any of the meat, nor did Ramapee. A religious thing, maybe.

"I would appreciate the chance to rest here a night or two," said Lura. "You are most gracious."

"You are the friend of my friends. Not only Xido but also Marana and Saj."

"They are in Lorj, aren't they? With those jewels — including the one

I gave them! I can sense them. Hmm, I wonder if I could speak afar with the boy. His abilities have grown." The woman shrugged. "I might try sometime."

Domi rose from her place. "I should see about preparing places for our guests," she said. "And for me and Sesa, for that matter. Perhaps — yes, the Lady Lura could have the upstairs room that is, um, ready." Her eyes turned to the four Ildin soldiers. "Do you need them close, my lady?"

"Anywhere and anything will do for all of us. We have been roughing it these past weeks, coming down from the mountains and then taking to the river. Ramapee, of course, will stay with me."

The girl hurried off to attend to it. The Cana watched her go, apparently with some amusement, before saying, "She is Marana's sister?"

"Half-sister. Lord Hurrum's natural daughter." How would she know this?

"She reminds me some of her." Lura turned her attention back to her meal. She had a considerable appetite. By the time she filled it, Domi had returned with an assistant, who escorted the men to their quarters. Each bowed reverentially to their leader before exiting.

"We'll have you just upstairs from the Lady Qala," she announced to Lura. "We can all go together."

By this time, Samee and her children had gone home, and Zedos had gone to sleep. Qala bundled him up and headed through the double doors into her manor house without further word.

Down the hall — the stairs lay ahead, Qala's rooms to the right. "Sesa and I can use the beds in the nursery, at least for tonight," said Domi. "I'll be with you shortly. This way." She led the guests up the stairway and Qala led Vasema to her own rooms.

"I'll put Zedos down in my bedroom for the night," she said. "Make yourself comfortable." By the time she had the boy in his bed, Domi had rejoined them and the two young women were conversing in low tones. They were likely to keep that up much of the night.

Domi looked up. "I think I am a little frightened of our guest," she said. "More than your gods even."

"She is a woman used to command," was Vasema's assessment.

85

"Like Qala."

"Yes," agreed Vasema. "They can both be scary."

"Maybe once," murmured Qala. "I am just a little dried-up old woman now."

Their looks did not suggest belief. "So, Sesa, what think you of Benaro's choice of wife?"

She did not even take time to consider the question. "They do make a good couple. They seem happy." She smirked at Domi. "And we must admit that Samee is prettier than either of us."

Her friend nodded agreement. Neither girl was vain. "And not the sort to put up with any nonsense from him either."

"Just what he needs. As we are for our own husbands, I might add."

"Absolutely. Isn't there wine here somewhere, my lady?"

There had better be. Ah, yes, a nearly full crock. She poured out a mug of the dark purplish-red liquid for each of them. It smelled slightly vinegary, but was sweet and strongly flavored.

"You do realize," she said, "Flawum is likely to name your husband a noble as soon as his kingdom is recognized."

Vasema turned to her friend, her look mingling surprise and delight. "Oh, you will be Lady Domi? I didn't know this. Or I just hadn't thought of it."

Domi was not nearly so delighted with the thought of being a noble-woman. "It would change our lives. I don't know if I want that. I'm happy here."

"I'll suggest the Viceroy name Corad as ambassador to Flawum's court," promised Qala. "Then you two could live together."

"A most excellent idea," said Vasema, lifting her mug in approval. "But I am not sure Sarowhem could get by without my presence."

"Nor Melawhem without mine," added Domi. "We are quite indispensable."

"And quite full of yourselves," Qala observed. "I suppose I was too at your age."

"Were you already a pirate?" asked Vasema.

Qala sipped her wine before answering. "On my way to becoming one." It was not a subject she wished to discuss.

"Someone must write down your story," the young noblewoman declared. "Neither of my parents!"

But she had, in fact, given much of it to Galana. Be that as it may. Galana — how fared she? Qala had pushed her concern for the woman into the back of her mind but now it returned.

"This Cana is a powerful sorceress," she said. "I wonder if she might help us in recovering your mother."

"That is a question I might also ask," spoke Xido, stepping from the shadows.

23.

"Mec Lura is Tesran, you know," said Xido. "She left the city before it fell to you Mura."

Centuries ago. Qala knew enough history to realize that. Xido went on, addressing the Cana now. "Qala spent time in Tesra, or so she once told me."

"A very long time ago. I was but a girl." It was no longer a great city then, but a place of ruins, a shadow of its former glory.

The sorceress and her attendant breakfasted with them in Qala's own chambers. "I have lived long among my adopted people," said Lura. "I no longer think of myself as Tesran." She looked toward Samee, helping the children with their meal. "You are of the Ildin, are you not?"

"Yes, m'lady. Um, sort of."

The Cana nodded. "Yes, sort of. I understand this. Your people have half-become Sharshites." She might have sighed, or perhaps only took a deep breath, before continuing. "The Ildin who once lived around here have fully become so and remember not their ancestors."

"Nor their gods," came Ramapee's soft voice.

"The gods can handle that, my girl," Xido assured her. "It is true that there is much Ildin blood among the common folk of this valley. An old shrine to Banat lies in the hills above Sarowhem."

"Where Saj and my sister began their adventure," said Domi. "When I was a child we were told it was haunted."

"Only by the priests of Munu who appropriated it. There is nothing much there, just a cave in the hillside."

"I would like to see it." Ramapee sounded wistful. She knew there would be no time, nor were she and her mistress likely to come back this way.

"The cave on your sacred mountain is more impressive."

"And it will all be blown to bits according to Saj, cave, mountain, valley," Lura reminded the god. "Thus we leave our home. Already I have accompanied many of our people across the mountains. The rest prepare for the journey."

"Into the great and mostly empty valley of the Veltar. Ildin have been filtering into its lower reaches for generations." He paused, seemingly intent on the filling of his stomach, before off-handedly adding, "And also across the straits to the isle of Lorj."

At last he brings up his mission, thought Qala. It was about time. "Where Saj and Marana now live. Did you see them?"

"And has Saj mastered the jewels?" asked Lura.

"To some extent. It seems my very old friend and onetime protege, the wizard Im, has given him lessons in their use." He grinned at the Tesran sorceress.

"My grandfather still lives? Why, he must be close to a thousand years!"

"Im dwells yet among the Ildin of Lorj. He retired to the temple of Banat there, high in the mountains. I hadn't the time to visit him but I shall."

"And does that demon of his yet follow him about? I do not think they would let it into the temple."

"Recently dead. Im misses it — he and Cory were together most of his life."

Qala was growing impatient with this chatter and reminiscing. "So did Saj have anything to say about the Lady Galana?"

"Not knowing the lady, he had no idea where to search. So I suggested he look into the Sea Stone and try to find your old friends, Qala."

She nodded. "We do suspect pirates of taking her."

"And correctly so. He discovered both pirates and prisoner. They have her somewhere near water. This he could tell. Maybe on a coast, maybe on an island, and definitely north of where he dwells in Lanlaz. He was always good at determining directions, wasn't he?" Qala had to admit that was so. He had located many a ship or storm for his pirate captors. "Not northwest so she is unlikely to be on Lorj itself."

"That remains a great deal of area. But Galana is well?" The knowledge she lived was welcome, to be sure, but Qala yearned to know more.

"So it seems. And remember Saj sees the future, not what is happening right now." Xido chuckled. "He also thanked me for saving his life while I was in crocodile form. Again. I would that I could remember either time myself!"

"You might be able to if you entered the Eyes with him," commented Lura.

"I'd rather not." His tone suggested he felt strongly about it. "One more thing — Galana is held in a house somewhere, not in a camp nor on a ship. Of this Saj was certain."

"I thank you for this," said Vasema. Tears glistened on her cheeks, but she spoke now in an even and determined voice. "So what is to be done with this knowledge?"

"We could send a messenger to Flawum's court," suggested Domi.

"Definitely," agreed Qala. But that seemed little. "I should go south," she decided. "We are dealing with people I know well." Perhaps even the pirates over whom she had once ruled.

"And I with you," stated Xido. He looked to the Cana.

The sorceress laughed. "I am traveling that way too. We might as well go together."

"But not you and I, Sesa," said Domi. "We are not equipped to meddle in this."

Qala agreed. Vasema was competent but would add nothing to the expedition. "And you, too, might be a target," she reminded the girl, "as both daughter to Vullum and wife to Corad. In fact, you might be safer back at Sarowhem."

Vasema looked decidedly sour about this but nodded an agreement. "I'll carry word of this back to Hurrum," she promised. "But I might return. I'd rather wait here for any news."

"Domi, you will be in charge, of course. I trust you to care for Zedos, Samee, as seems best to you."

"Yes, m'lady. Um, what if the boy disappears again? Or, you know, any of that sort of thing?"

"You might do better to bring him along," said Xido. "I could keep an eye out for 'that sort of thing.'" The god seemed to think on that for a moment. "Or send him to stay with my brother."

Budo as babysitter? Qala thought not. "Very well, we bring Zedos with us. He's old enough to travel. And, mmm, Damana too, as his nurse. If she is willing." And maybe Augun. He could be useful. "Tomorrow morning. Does anyone want that last piece of bacon?"

90

24.

"He has your jaw," remarked the Cana, "and your cheekbones. Indeed, he favors you much more than his father." She gave Qala an enigmatic smile. "At least the part that we can see."

Nor was Zedos as dark as Xido, though still quite brown. His hair had grown out black and wavy. At the moment, he rode before his mother, clinging to the reins as though he were master of this steed. All their rides were from Qala's own stables; she had insisted the Ildin have horses and not slow them down.

The boy should learn to truly ride soon. A small pony. And he must learn to sail and to swim and, eventually, the ways of a blade. So much in his future!

A future that would be not be as most expected, the men and women living their lives as they ever had, expecting tomorrow to be as yesterday. Changes were coming. This sorceress riding at her side knew it. Xido knew it. Saj had seen some of it.

All of this played a part in that future. Flawum's new kingdom. His new life, for that matter, and those of his offspring in two worlds. The Cana's people. Marana and Saj and their children. Her son. All she could do is prepare him for it, rear him as best she was able.

"Giyee-up!" called out Zedos. "Gonna see tah king!" He tipped his little head sideways, as if examining something none of the rest of them could see. "Jong daddy!"

"Well," remarked Lura. "I wonder how he figured that one out."

Ir might have mentioned it in his presence, or some other being in that world. He could even have overheard it in his own home. Still, it was surprising he would remember and understand it.

"It is not just to find Ildin you ride south, is it?" asked Qala.

"I felt a need. It might have something to do with Xido. No, no, it certainly has something to do with Xido. Probably the Ildin gods are a part of it too."

"But not the gods of Xido's world?" They had certainly gotten involved in her own life.

"They do not seem to concern themselves much with such things. Even Xido cares more about individuals than he does about the human race." She gave Qala a knowing smile. "Individuals such as you. The gods can see in you what men may not."

The Mur could not imagine what that might be. "What of these Ildin gods? I know little about them."

"All quite conscientious deities, even the evil ones, ready to do their duty. Most don't see humans as an important part of that duty but they bother themselves with us now and again. Banat is different. He is interested in us and where we are going."

"Xido mentioned him. He felt he might be arranging things behind the scenes."

"Quite likely. Banat sees what may be." They rode on without speaking for a minute or two. Qala could feel her son falling asleep. No problem; he was securely tied to her, with a silk scarf about his middle. The roads were still good here, half a day's ride south from River Chas. Qala knew they were less traveled, less well kept up, further along.

Lura spoke, taking up their conversation again. "Somehow, over the eons, Xido and Banat have become friends. Xido does like to get away from his own world, of course, and see what is going on elsewhere."

"Have you met this god?"

"No, never. Once Kamat appeared to me, asking me to lead his followers. Most of what I know I have learned from our Xit."

"My Muram gods do not get involved with mortals very much."

"Nor do the gods of Tesra. But they exist. They all exist." Lura raised her eyes to the riders ahead of them. "Your maid is not used to long rides. She will be sore tonight."

Serve her right, thought Qala for just a second and then as quickly regretted it. She surely had no reason for jealousy. After all, she felt none toward this Tesran at her side, a woman who had known Xido far longer and more intimately than ever she had. If anything, it was the trickster god himself toward whom she felt resentment. He had come close to abusing her hospitality.

Ramapee rode silently beside Damana, behind Augun and a lad from her estate. The Cana's four men brought up the rear. Xido had hung back with them all morning, chatting about something. As the conversation was in Ildin, Qala had no idea what.

"She seems a nice girl," Lura went on. "Attractive, too."

"And headstrong and inclined to throw herself at any man who comes along." But it was true. Damana had at least the attractiveness of youth. As her brother, she was compact and solid. She would probably tend to fat someday. Freckles were sprinkled across her cheeks, below coarse brown hair, bleached to a straw color by the sun and cropped short.

Maybe she was even attracted herself, some. Could that be why she had felt that way about her and Xido? No, no. That would be ridiculous. But maybe she had felt protective of her.

"Hmm," was all the Cana had in response. Qala suspected she could have said much more.

"Men ahead!" called out Augun. "Soldiers."

There was no ducking them, nor any reason this close to home. A half-troop of Muram lancers came up the road. Both groups halted and their sergeant rode forward, a squat fellow with a sparse black beard. "Who leads here? Identify yourselves!"

She knew this Mur already. "I greet you, Sergeant Pargom." She allowed herself to advance half a horse's length.

The leader gave her a salute. "Oh, I didn't see you, ma'am. My greetings to you. It's the Lady Qala," he tossed back over his shoulder to his troop." They all know her name and her estate, and their patrols carried them there at times. "It's good to have Mura such as you holding things down here on this frontier, ma'am." His eyes swept across the rest of the party. The Mur's approval did not seem to extend to them.

"And you and your men are always welcome at Melawhem." She waved an arm toward her companions. "I am escorting these Ildin priestesses south. It wouldn't do for them to travel alone."

"Not safe for anyone, further on. Can't trust that Pretender."

"But my friend Admiral Murgom is at his court even now."

"So it is said, ma'am. But take care." He saluted again and led his men north.

"He is right, of course," said Qala, watching them disappear in the dust of a summer road. "It won't be safe further along. Your men should get their swords out their packs, my Lady Lura."

"Indeed. And their bows too." She looked toward Augun and the young Sharshite. "Are your men handy with weapons?"

"Augun is a fair hand with a sword. The boy Horos is raw yet but one of those I have been training." Something Ranwif would be attending to — should be attending to — were he not running off to Flawum's court so frequently. Horos did show ability. Maybe he could train as an equester. "He has traveled south before with my master of arms. That is why he is with us."

"Let's move on," suggested Xido. "We have hours yet today." She signaled Augun to again lead the way.

They camped that night in a field by the road, no tents, no fire, only their blankets and a cold meal. It was not necessary to hurry so, maybe, but neither was there a reason to dawdle.

"Oh, I wish I were in my bed!" moaned Damana.

"Beds are to be born in and to die in," Qala told her. "Avoid them otherwise."

"An old Muram proverb! I haven't heard it in centuries," laughed Lura. "And I must say, I have found some rather pleasant uses for beds."

The Sharshite girl grinned. "That is so, my lady. I wish I were in my bed and had someone to share it!"

Qala could only shake her head — in part, to hide her own amusement. She didn't mind sleeping on the ground. It was dry, the night was warm. In a year or two, if all went well, there might be inns along this road. An investment to consider!

Zedos had settled down without complaint by her side. She needn't worry about him. There would be sentries through the night. There was Xido. Tomorrow they would ride on toward the court of Flawum, as she had nearly two years ago with a different set of companions — Ranwif, Corad, Sesa — and with the assistance of Xido's siblings.

A moment later, it was morning and someone was gently shaking her awake.

25.

The first thing she noticed was that Xido was missing. Off to take a piss, Qala assumed at first, but he did not return. "Do we wait for him?" she finally asked the others. All was ready for them to ride on, otherwise.

"He can find us," felt the Cana. Qala was inclined to agree.

"Very well," she said. "Let's ride." Xido's horse was led by one of the Ildin. Those four were all well-armed now, short swords at their hips, recurved bows on their backs.

Damana rode beside her mistress this morning, a sleeping Zedos slung across her back. Lura trotted along beyond the girl, Ramapee following and seemingly lost in her own thoughts.

"Yon guardsman is a handsome young fellow," commented the sorceress.

"Oh, Horos is scared of girls," Damana replied.

"It doesn't keep him from taking looks at you." Which was true. Qala had noted it too, but preferred discretion.

The girl only shrugged. "Well," said Lura, "that is your loss. Were I a couple hundred years younger — hmm, maybe anyway."

From the corner of her eye, Qala could see the Ildin priestess shaking her head, but not without a hint of amusement in her expression. Not the sort to enter into such banter herself, Qala recognized.

Later, as she rode close to the Cana she whispered, "Maybe it is your Ramapee and my Horos you should be trying to bring together. They seem two of a kind."

Her suggestion brought another of Lura's enigmatic smiles. "Most unlikely, my friend. He is not at all her type."

Qala could only shrug. The woman knew her companion better than she. "I wonder where Xido is."

"His home would be the best guess. Is it true you visited it?"

"I did. Not when he was there, of course. And I came back through the gate located not far from here."

"It is rare for any but sorcerers to know of such things."

"I had no choice but to learn!"

"I wish I could glimpse that world," sighed the Cana. "Other than visiting it in wizard fashion, seeing but not fully there. To walk amid such terrible beauty! And you met his brother and sister too."

"Both brothers." On an impulse, she leaned in and whispered. "Xido is a better lover than either — but Mawa is best of all."

Lura only nodded. "As I said before, the gods see in you what men do not."

The next morning, Xido was again in camp, as if he had never been away. "Your report on little Jong's abilities led me to go visit her and her mother. Ir was quite distraught when Mong came back to her with an incoherent tale of monsters. Not that mafadwi are ever very coherent." The slightest twist of smile before he continued. "It gave me a chance to look at all Flawum's children."

"Any dangers there, you think?" asked Lura.

"They are all unusual. But I believe only Jong will ever travel between worlds, as do I. As do gods. Mong's bond to Zedos may allow him to continue to travel to this world, or that might fade. There's no telling. Still not bothering with a fire? I could use some hot food."

"When we reach Flawum's keep," Qala told him. "He does not have good memories of you, does he?"

"I did help Marana and Saj steal the jewel from his crown. Perhaps I could shape-shift a little."

"Always risky," felt Lura.

"Yes. I'll just ride on in with the rest of you and take my chances. And maybe get that meal."

"Then saddle up. Horos is eager to go now that he gets to lead."

"Both of us know that way as well as he," said Xido.

"But he has ridden it more recently."

They drew near to a good-sized stream, a major tributary of Chas, that day and then veered away from it again. "I hear it is too wild for navigation," commented Qala. "That's too bad. A waterway south would be useful."

"Dams could tame the lower stretches, not that I would want to see them." Xido scanned the road southward. "I suspect a canal could be run through the swamplands to join Chas and Arlak as well. That will happen no time soon."

"Thank one god or another for that!" It would not be good for trade on her part of the river at all. "We used to hear rumors of smugglers having secret ways through the swamps."

"That will no longer be worth the effort."

True enough. They rode on through the afternoon, a little more leisurely than the previous days. It was not good to push the horses, nor themselves for that matter. The terrain gradually grew a little more rolling. Flawum's keep was nestled in the low hills further south, the watershed between the valleys of the Chas and the Arlak.

Once it had commanded the best passage through those hills, and the lands around it had prospered. No more. The former Pretender certainly hoped for a return to those days.

Qala again had her son before her. Zedos alternately napped and fussed. He had had enough of this traveling and so had she. They should have stayed home. It was impetuous of her to head south, unbecoming for a woman her age, and a mother, to boot.

But if the centuries-old woman beside her could manage, so would she! What was that glint ahead, amid the roadside brush? Her training came to the fore at once. "Ambush!" she cried out.

Swords slid from scabbards; bows were nocked. How could she fight with Zedos strapped to her? She would have to hold back. None the less, Qala's curved sword was in her hand. Men on foot streamed from the undergrowth to grab at the horses, impede them and their riders, while mounted fighters, the ones whose armor she had spotted, broke into the open ahead. They outnumbered her party, two to one at least.

What? Something felt different of a sudden. Qala looked down. Zedos had vanished. Smart boy! Forward she rode and into the fray.

26.

What these attackers did not know was their intended victims included both a god and one of the most powerful sorcerers alive. The dead ones, of course, are mostly harmless.

"Goxo! Defend!" Lura cried out and at once one of her warriors rode to her side, sword bared. The other three were already loosing arrows as they could and, when they couldn't, drew their blades.

Xido took no time for any finesse of magic but waded into the enemy, sword swinging. On the second or third swing, the sword shattered on an opponent's armor. Qala could see him mouth an oath of some sort. He is too strong, she realized. It was more than the blade could handle. This was not the Xido she had known before.

It was to be noted that the man he had struck fell from his mount and did not get up again. Undeterred, the god attacked the next man he reached with his bare hands, eluding the fellow's clumsy swing of his sword. Or maybe Xido's quickness only made it look clumsy. Qala herself swung her sword to both sides, beating back those who dared get close.

One assailant, a squinty-eyed villain, had hold of Damana's bridle. From the look of him, he was already considering the rewards to follow a victory, leering up at her. Qala spurred her horse their direction.

Horos beat her, practically decapitating the man with one swing of his long sword. The boy had been paying attention to his lessons! Her horse shied suddenly, as something flared to her left. Fire, seeming to come from nowhere but obviously directed by the Cana. Pulled from some other world. Qala knew how that worked. "Settle down, boy," she murmured, bringing her steed back under control. She could see Xido on the other side of the melee literally throwing a man through the air.

Soon the rest of the attackers were flying too, in a different sense, flying away from the contest and into the woods. At least half a dozen lay dead or wounded. Any of theirs? Lura had dismounted and was examining one of her own followers.

"Persale will ride no further," she told the other Ildin who had gathered about her. Everyone else seemed to be intact, if a bit worse for wear. No, where was the Ildin girl? Ramapee. Qala surveyed the battlefield before her and then slowly turned around to see her sitting her mount quietly, close behind her.

"Behind you seemed the safest place to be, my lady," she said, with a smile nearly as enigmatic as that of her mistress. "Now I should see if I can be of use," she continued, dismounting. "I am trained in the arts of medicine."

Qala slid down from her own mount. The dun gelding had done well, despite never facing combat before. "Good lad," she said, patting him. "Let's see what we have here." She led him along, examining the fallen enemies. Men of the sea, mostly, by their clothing, by their weapons, by their very look. Pirates or smugglers.

How did they know they would be on this road? For that matter, how would they know there was any reason to stop them? Their information was secret, known to only a few, though others might have surmised they knew something of importance.

And the leaders of these pirates — if they were such — might recognize that Qala could be a danger to them. But, again, how would they know she traveled south? Her eyes lingered a moment on Augun. He could relay such information. But no, she did not believe it of him. The burly Mur had taken little harm in the fight.

Not so Xido. He was bloody and battered. She almost tripped over one of the attackers as she hurried toward him. The man groaned. Qala crouched beside him. A thrust through the gut. He would not survive nor even be able to answer questions. She slit his throat and rose to move on.

Only to notice many eyes on her, and a few shocked expressions. They did not know who she had been. Who she was still, really, Qala the Queen of Pirates. She could only shrug and go on to Xido. But she did try to keep her horse from trampling on the body. The fallen deserved respect.

"Are you hurt badly?" she asked the god. He looked it.

"Were I a man, I might be. This will heal quickly. More quickly were I to go home but quickly enough anyway." A wince was followed by a laugh. "When you knew little Xit the Sorcerer before, these wounds might have been more serious."

"Could you have been — slain?"

"I could have been badly hurt. Incapacitated for a long while. Whether I can be killed at all, in any form, I'm not really sure. It hasn't happened so far, anyway." He gave her a looking over. "It is good you had no hurt, Qala. When I get cleaned up and sorted out, I'll see if I can locate our son. I suspect he is quite safe."

She only nodded. The three Ildin men were chopping branches from the trees with their short swords. They mean to cremate their comrade, she realized. The other fallen? Best to get them off the road but no reason to do any more. They could have their own version of sky burial. More than a few appeared Muram anyway.

Once the dead were attended to, they moved down the road half a league and set up camp. For the first time, a fire was built. That is, Qala permitted it. She was the leader here. Not Xit, not the Cana.

"Zedos is safe," Xido had whispered to her as they rode from the scene of their skirmish. "I have spoken with my brother." Qala did not bother to ask which one. It did not matter.

Nothing seemed to matter at the moment. Except Zedos. He was the one thing that kept her tied to hope, kept her from the old paths of despair and emptiness. She could live for him when she could not live for herself.

It was near dark when a strange shape loomed up beyond the camp-fire's illumination, a bulky shadow with some bizarre misshapen head protruding above it. A moment later, Budo walked into the light with Zedos riding on his broad shoulders.

The god handed him down to his mother and took a seat on the ground. "He showed up in tears at my cave. I was not there, only a mortal woman who serves me, but she managed to calm him down." He turned his gaze toward his brother. "Despite not having many words, Zedos has the same gift of understanding tongues we do."

"And the mafadwi."

"I wondered about that when I was in your world," said Qala. "Only the humans couldn't speak with me."

"We don't understand it ourselves," Xido told her.

Budo chuckled, a deep resonant chuckle. "But that doesn't keep Mawa and Lenco from arguing about it."

"Oh, they have many theories. We thank you, Budo, for bringing the boy back."

"It probably won't be the last time," said the big god, rising. "I'd best be on my way." He stepped into the shadows of the evening and, undoubtedly, disappeared from the world.

"We need to be on our way too, in the morning," spoke Qala. "So a good night's sleep for you and me, my boy. Let's go find our blankets."

"Um-huh, Mommy. Giss you."

"Yes, Zedos. Kiss me and then sleep." And let tomorrow bring what it would. Let tomorrow bring its journeys and its destinations.

Part III.
A KING BY ANOTHER NAME

27.

It would be a stretch to call this town bustling, but it was much more alive than when last Qala had seen it. Then it seemed half-deserted. Still shabby, to be sure. They rode up the cobblestone street toward Flawum's keep.

"Change is in the air," said Lura.

"And change can bring profit," she replied. That was what drew people here now. The new king — who was the old king with a different title — would have concessions to award, trade agreements to work out. She might want to look into such things herself as long as she was here.

They had passed without problem into Flawum's realm. Horos was recognized. Qala herself was known to some as a friend of the king. The soon-to-be Celos of Arlacana. "We should first present ourselves to Flawum," said Qala. She looked toward the sun, nearing its zenith. "He may still be holding court."

"His habits have changed, my lady," Horos put in. It was rare he spoke to her, or to anyone, other than to occasionally give a terse command. He was a shy lad, to be sure.

And one Damana seemed to be seeing with new eyes since he had rescued her a few days ago. That would go as it would. Best she keep out of the way.

She nodded. Flawum had changed, it was true, and so undoubtedly had his habits. "He might or might not be willing to put us all up." They rode without challenge through the open gates, one of the guards giving Horos a wave.

Someone else waving on the steps leading up to the big double doors of the main entrance. These were thrown open, as usual. Ranwif. News of their presence would have preceded them. And the messenger Qala had sent preceded that, giving the court of Flawum notice of their journey south.

Ranwif turned a curious eye toward the Ildin but asked no question. "The celos is still holding morning audience," he informed Qala. "You might as well come in and be introduced. All of you."

That was something more than a request. The boy had some authority here. Yes, he would be leaving her soon. Qala did not doubt this. Grooms came and took charge of their animals.

She well knew the way to the throne room and led them forward, Ranwif and Horos flanking her. Left as soon as one entered and down a hallway. Glass windows, mostly intact, brought in light on the one side; the audience chamber opened on the other. Flawum was near the end of his day's business, it appeared, with few remaining in the room and his own attention turned to a sheaf of papers he held, while some minister or another pointed out things in them.

"Qala!" he cried out when he spied her at the door. "Come in. Do come in." He rose from his throne, a simple high-backed wooden chair, tossing the documents aside, and surveyed those who trailed in behind her.

His eyes lit on the man standing nonchalantly at her side. "Xit? I hardly expected to see you again!"

"He is not quite who you think he is, your majesty," spoke Qala, stepping forward. "He is brother to those you met on our little expedition. Mawa and Lenco and Budo."

"Oh!" He scrutinized Xido. "Hmm, yes I can see it." Truly see it, Qala suspected, see the godhood in the wiry dark man standing before him. Neither would say anything of that in public. "Well, I can surmise why you have come, my lady, and we can discuss that later. So who are your companions?"

"Ildin priestesses and their attendants, traveling south," Qala said. She could give more detail in private. Those gathered here need know no more. "And my own attendants. My Lord Flawum knows Horos, I believe."

The king nodded toward the boy and shifted his attention to Damana.

"That is your son the girl carries? He has grown! You must meet my own little girls. A sweeter pair never were!"

Flawum looked to be in the most excellent of health. He had grown his beard out. It was quite luxuriant and darker than his dirty-blond hair. He waved one of his attendants to him. "Find them rooms. All of them," he ordered. "And no skimping on their accommodations! However many rooms they say they need." Looking back to Qala, he said, "You will of course be my guests."

"Thank you, your highness."

Xido whispered, "Back out. Seven steps, then turn."

"No longer necessary," Ranwif whispered back. "Protocol has changed." He simply bowed to the king and turned. The rest did as he had.

"I hardly recognize the man," remarked Xido when they reached the hall outside.

"Time in your world awakened something in him. Now how many rooms do we need? Damana and Zedos are with me, of course." They had returned to the main hallway and stood before a wide stair.

Flawum's man nodded, though he probably did not know whom she meant. "Would you wish to be close to the admiral, madame?"

"Not usually. Is he on the second floor?"

"Ground floor. Down that way," Ranwif told her, gesturing toward the far end of the hall. Past Flawum's own apartments. "Vullum and Corad are upstairs."

She leaned in and whispered, "Has a demand come to Vullum?"

"It has. He will wish to see you."

"Put us on the second floor," she told the attendant. It would make matters easier if she wished to speak with the two Sharshite nobles, without Murgom's presence.

The man conferred with another servant for a few moments, nodded. "This way," he announced, starting up the staircase, while Ranwif headed off to some other business. The palace was still a dingy place, and in need of maintenance. Most of the plaster had long cracked and fallen from the stone walls. Upkeep would be less of a priority up here. Where was the room she and her companions had occupied before? To the right at the top of the stairs, as she remembered.

They were led to the left. "There should be four rooms ready over here, madame." He looked over the group. "Will that be enough?"

"As long as there are enough beds you could stuff us all in one apart-ment."

"I'll room with Ranwif," Horos announced. He probably had on previous visits.

She considered the young man. "No," she told him. "I want you close. Remember it is I you serve."

"Yes, ma'am," he mumbled. He might have reddened slightly, embar-rassed to have misspoken. The passageway was dark so it was hard to say.

The rooms proved to be together, two on each side of the hall. Long unused and dusty. Windowless, too. Three would have been enough, or even two. They were all of about the same size, certainly large enough. "We'll be in here," she decided, looking into one. "The Cana and Ramapee next to us. You men decide how to apportion yourselves across the hall."

Lura did that for them. She pointed to the door opposite hers and her warriors entered the room. "I guess the other one is ours," Xido told Horos and Augun. "Now all I need is some lunch before my nap."

28.

"I had never seen Budo before he visited our camp."

"I am not surprised, Lura. He and Xido did not get along well before."

"Oh, I could see big Budo was only tolerating his brother. Mostly because of you and your son, I think. Xido has been unkind to him in the past — this I know."

The two quietly conversed in a corner of Qala's room. Damana and Zedos occupied the two beds, both asleep. It seemed the entire keep took the siesta; little was stirring when they had returned from the kitchens. Not that anyone much occupied this floor. There were soldiers quartered on the next one up and, it was rumored, a few prisoners. Above that were attics and turrets and parapets, all somewhat haphazardly arranged by Qala's judgment. She wouldn't want to defend the place.

But it was not built as a fortress, she had been told. It was a palace, a country retreat of the Sharshite royal family, repurposed when a scion of that family fled to these hills and proclaimed himself Ri — the first Pretender.

A polite rap on the door. Whoever it was might think them sleeping. Qala opened it to Ranwif and Corad. She looked back over her shoulder at the sleepers. "Let's talk in Xido's room," she said, slipping out. "Do you wish to come, my lady?" she asked the Cana. The woman only shook her head.

"Vullum is not with you?"

"Murgom is keeping him busy," replied the nobleman.

"But Lord Corad was able to escape the admiral."

"Elude, might be more correct. You would know the apartments Murgom occupies, Qala. Flawum's wife dwelt there before."

The lady-in-waiting who waited just long enough to wed a king. "How is the Lady Hasala?"

"Well and happy and pregnant again."

The door opened before they reached it, Horos peering out at the trio. He stepped aside wordlessly to let them enter.

And carefully checked the hall before closing up again. Qala approved.

"This is like old times," spoke Corad. "We lack only my wife."

"Who I hope is staying safely at home," replied Qala, and proceeded to fill him and Ranwif in on all that had happened since they left. Leaving out, to be sure, any mention of what she and Galana had been up to.

"Things have moved more slowly here," the nobleman said at the conclusion of her tale. "We work out the various little details of our accord, when Murgom is sober and Flawum isn't distracted. Some days nothing gets done — and then word came of Lady Galana."

"And a message has come to Vullum, I understand." There wasn't any wine in these rooms, was there? Someone should remedy that.

"Telling him to abandon the negotiations."

"Will he?" asked Xido, who hadn't seemed to be paying any attention. He and Augun had been rolling dice on one of the beds.

"Vullum may love his wife but is too attached to doing his duty to let her kidnapping get in the way."

"Maybe," said the god. "Maybe not. He has not yet had to truly choose. Ha, I hit my number!"

Augun raised his eyes to his mistress. "Is this fellow an honest player?"

"Probably. But I'd watch him carefully anyway."

"Yes," said Xido, grinning. "I might do something like this."

Both dice jumped, seemingly on their own.

Maybe the burly Mur jumped a little as well, despite himself. "Grand-mother!" he rasped.

Qala had to laugh. It was an oath children would use, rather than grown men — much less pirates. "You reached around through another world to do that, didn't you?"

He spread his arms. "My secrets have been revealed." He turned back to Augun. "It's too difficult to finesse. Too obvious. Were I to cheat I would use ordinary human methods."

And probably use them well. "So," she asked Corad, "when do we meet with your fellow diplomats?"

"We are all to have supper tonight with Flawum. Those I feel should be invited; they tend to leave that sort of detail to me. You Qala, to be sure. I think I should include Xit. My, you have changed since last I spied you, my friend."

"Yes, I hear he was quite scaly then," commented Qala.

"And when our friend Nedos saw him too. Oh, Nedos is here. He'll be with us tonight. Hmm, should we invite any others, Lady Qala?"

"The Mec Lura, if she is willing to come."

"Mec Lura — why, she is the Cana, is she not? The Sorceress of the Mountains?"

"That she is," Xido told him. "And I would not be inclined to offend her."

"Very well. The three of you then." He considered young Ranwif for a moment. "Probably no reason for you to be there, my boy."

"Thank Jov for that. Horos," he called, "dine with me tonight and we'll catch up. You too, Augun."

That wouldn't do. "Not if it means leaving Zedos unguarded," stated Qala.

"Then we'll bring him and my sister along," said Ranwif. "The Ildin girl too, if her mistress doesn't need her."

"Sister?" asked Xido.

"I consider her and Benaro to be my brother and sister. Their family took me in when mine was murdered."

"Ah." The god chuckled. "It is good to be able to choose ones own siblings."

"So, I'll be back in an hour or two," spoke Corad. "You will have to tell your story all over again then."

There was really nothing to add to the message they had sent before them. There was no point in coming here at all. Qala silently cursed herself for leaving her home, for accepting a responsibility for Galana. She should care only about Zedos.

She felt the anger rising in her, the anger toward herself, the anger toward the world, that she might once have turned outward. That won't do, she told herself. Let it go. The old roads of self-hatred and despair should not be trodden again. Let your son be reason enough to exist.

Xido was watching her. He understood. He knew how she struggled to go on sometimes, in the days when she had been alone. Alone even though she ruled as a queen. Sometimes, back then, simply getting from dawn to sundown was a victory. And other times — oh, other times! Then surviving the day became a struggle for those around her, not knowing whom she might lash out at.

"At least I brought a gown," was the only reply she had.

29

"They took my jewel too, your majesty, though I handed it over will-ingly," said Lura.

"You would not be where you are today," Xido told him, "had it not occurred. That theft started things moving, the first of a series events."

Corad raised an eyebrow at this. "Would not my sister running off with Saj be the first?"

"That, in and of itself, was meaningless, as was all that led up to it. They could have headed off to Lorj right then and none of these things would have happened."

"But they decided otherwise."

"And that made the difference. Once we had the Earth Stone – your crown jewel, sir – one thing led to another."

"Fate?" asked the king.

Xido wrinkled his nose. "I do not like that word. But in your case it might be apt."

Flawum's laugh came easy and unaffected. "I like to think I have a fate. Perhaps only to live happily with my queen from now on."

"Will the Lady Hasala be joining us?" asked Qala. Where was the server? Oh, there. She held up her goblet to signal for more wine.

"Not feeling well this evening. That's common in pregnancy, isn't it?" He did not wait for answers but pushed onward. "Do come by and see her in the morning. Bring your son!"

"Yes, your majesty," she murmured, taking a sip from her replenished goblet. It was mediocre wine at best, a potent but somewhat flavorless red, probably from the sunny vineyards of Lorj. They could use some sun in here. Flawum's dining room was another of the windowless spaces in this palace. At least there were plenty of lamps around the room, and bright tapestries.

It was like Murgom, used to being master of all around him when at sea, to keep the king waiting. Could he also hope to achieve some subtle advantage in his negotiations? That might work on some men but Qala doubted Flawum even noted it. There, at last, the admiral rolling through the doorway, seemingly in serious conversation with Lord Vullum. Close behind scuttled Flawum's chief minister, attempting to make himself part of the discussion. What was his name? Had she ever heard it?

Captain Nedos followed, a more than slightly amused expression on his face. No longer a captain of the Muram navy was he, but on his way to being a successful merchant captain. Already there, perhaps. Once she preyed on such as Nedos, plundered their ships, enslaved their crews. Qala in no way regretted this; her past allowed her present. It created it.

All blurred. A knife appeared in the hand of a servant. No, not a servant, one of Flawum's guardsmen. The man lunged toward Admiral Murgom. Those about the table reacted, some starting to rise, some staring in momentary inaction. Qala was on her feet, her own knife in hand — one of her knives — without thinking. Something flew by her, another blur, a shining golden blur, followed by a body.

The assassin staggered, knife slicing the air nowhere near the intended victim. In another moment, Xido was on him, knocking him to the floor. A goblet lay on the ground beside him. Why, the god had thrown it at the man and struck him true. True enough.

"A good cast," spoke Murgom. He squinted at his savior. "Xit, isn't it? I was told you were here."

By then, all had gathered around the scene — all save Lura who sipped wine still, unperturbed. "One of my own?" wondered Flawum. A sergeant of the guard appeared, taking in the tableau. "Take this man, um, upstairs," the king ordered. "We'll find out what is what later."

The attacker had regained his wind. "Death to the Mura!" he cried out. "I sought only to serve you, your highness. To save you."

"Ah." Flawum shook his head. "One of those. Go ahead," he told the sergeant and turned back to his guests. "Maybe we can eat now."

"Excellent idea," felt Murgom. He slipped his own knife back into its sheath. The admiral had drawn almost as quickly as Qala. She would not have been surprised had he managed to defend himself without aid.

But neither matched Xido. How could they? His speed, his skill, his strength were beyond human ability. Not greatly, perhaps, yet enough.

"Be wareful of the wine on the floor," spoke Flawum, leading the way back to the table. "It seems our Xit threw a full goblet."

"Quite wasteful," noted Murgom. Neither asking nor being shown to a seat, he took a place at Flawum's right hand. The Cana, as the ranking woman there — the only other woman there, in truth — sat opposite. He peered across the table, possibly trying to tell if he knew her.

"May I present the Lady Lura?" spoke the king. "This is Murgom, admiral and envoy. I believe the rest of us all know each other? Oh, Lord Vullum, my lady." He nodded in the general direction of the Sharshite noble, who had taken a place beside Corad near the other end of the table.

"And me, your highness," added Nedos. "I shall present myself. Captain Nedos, at your service."

"Husband to Kataree." The sorceress smiled, as enigmatically as ever. "I have conversed with your wife, Captain. Only recently, when I learned of things that had happened on Lorj." Her eyes flickered to Xido for but a moment.

"We must have more of that story," said Xido. "But what brings you to the court of the celos, Captain?"

"Oh, I was asked to look over Arlacas. I know the area well."

And might be looking to trade there himself, Qala told herself. "I know the town some," she offered, as offhandedly as she could manage.

"Did business there, I would guess," replied the sailor. "Ah, that's welcome." He drank deeply of his wine. "I hope this came north on one of my ships."

"Not at your prices, my dear captain," said Flawum.

"All that is likely to change."

"Indeed so. No more trading with smugglers — and worse." Qala thought for a moment he would look toward her. But no, the king knew nothing of her past.

Nedos nodded his agreement. "The Pirate King is definitely unhappy about this. We have heard things."

"Their new leader," said Xido, with a completely straight face and not the least of a glance in her direction. "Know you his name?"

"It is reported he goes by Quso."

Flawum was puzzled by the name. "Muram?"

"I believe so." Nedos did not sound completely sure. "Most of the pirates are Mura."

Qala could not keep from laughing. "He is Muram indeed, though it be not the name he was born with. It means 'piss,' more or less."

"You know the man, Lady Qala?" asked Nedos.

"I do. Or did. Always more a politician than a leader of men," she said.

Flawum was taking all this in, seemingly more interested than surprised by any of it. "I suspect your knowledge could be of use to us. And you bring other knowledge, too, do you not? Knowledge of Lord Vullum's wife."

"That is so, sir," said Xido.

"And we shall hear it all. But first, here comes the roast!"

30.

As Flawum and Murgom wanted to talk, Vullum and Corad had little choice but to remain. The other guests made their goodbyes to the king and their way to the stairs.

"Just the fact of the attempt might put the negotiations on rocky ground," Nedos was saying.

The others doubted this. "Murgom probably enjoyed the excitement," felt Qala.

"Maybe so," admitted the sailor. "You say you know this Quso?"

"I do. In fact, I believe my man Augun sailed with him." She didn't just believe — she knew. He had been mate on Quso's ship. That disturbed her, brought back those suspicions she had dismissed.

There was no point in thinking about that now. "Come on to our quarters and visit a while," she said. "Maybe you can give us your tale."

Nedos gave her a courtly little bow. "I might, if you ply me with enough wine, my lady."

"If we ply you with much more wine you're likely to forget it," muttered Xido.

The door to the Ildin warriors' room stood open, with the three men and Augun sitting in a circle on the floor. "Oh, my lady," said the Mur, rising when he glimpsed them at the entry, "these lads was teaching me one of their games. Everyone else is in your room. I, um, made sure the door was open so I could keep an eye out, like."

"Good man," Qala said. "No need to stop playing." He may have felt uncomfortable staying with those young people but he was conscientious enough to watch out for them. Augun resumed his game as the others followed her to her own quarters.

There were the five they expected — and two others. "We never get invited to parties," said Lenco.

Mawa added to the complaint. "Yes, why do mortals prefer our brother?"

Lenco nodded. "He's every bit as likely to eat one of them as we are."

"If you liked mortals," spat out Xido, "they might like you a little more."

"We like *some* mortals," objected Mawa.

"But we find it hard to take them as seriously as you." Lenco might have even sounded a little hurt. Qala could not guess whether it was sincere. Yet it was true. These sibling gods found it hard to take anything seriously for very long. They were too wrapped up in their own world, their own immortality.

"He seems to be mortal," said Mawa, gently inclining her head in the direction of a sleepy Zedos, in Damana's arms. "But a powerful little mortal."

"That is certain," spoke Lura. She seemed happy to see her aide sitting here, giving her a quick smile. Ramapee was a little older than the others and did not seem very outgoing. Qala would not have been surprised had she chosen to be alone in her own room. "You can see the other form in the boy, can you not?"

Xido turned to her, not quite in astonishment but certainly surprised. "I could sense something, but it is hidden, integrated into who he is." His eyes returned to his son. "He is as a mafadwi, in a way, for he can not separate his natures."

"So far," replied the Cana.

Mawa and Lenco exchanged a look that dripped with hidden meanings. "Can you see his other form?" asked the goddess.

"It is that of a bird, with feathers of flame."

"The shape of our grandfather," breathed Lenco.

"The Firebird himself. Can you show me?" asked Xido.

"Come." Lura held out her hands. Qala was pretty sure physical contact was not necessary for what these powerful beings were about to attempt but maybe it helped in some way. All three gods joined the sorceress. "This won't work for any of the rest of you," she apologized, "so pardon us if we go elsewhere for a minute or two."

Then all four stood there, unmoving, eyes unfocused, in the uncomfortable silence of the room. Nedos was surely quite lost amid this. Maybe Horos too, though he might have been filled in some by now. "Is there wine?" asked Qala.

It was Ramapee who rose to pour her a goblet. The young woman was undoubtedly quite used to the sort of thing in which her mistress was engaged. "You have no gift yourself, I take it," the Muram woman murmured.

"No, Lady Qala. I am a priestess and nothing more."

"Qala, only." She had been telling too many people that, for far too long. The pale wine was passable but had the odd spicy flavor of the grapes native to the region, the wild vines that grew everywhere. Qala had been assured she was better off growing other varieties. "They are returning."

Lenco shook himself. "Yes," he said, "a firebird, but not fully formed."

"I am surprised he has no crocodile in him," said Qala. "He certainly took to water at once."

Xido chuckled at that. "It is in him but it, too, remains unformed. How about some of that wine for us?"

As the Ildin girl poured for him and the others, he continued, "The gods — those of our world — are able to some degree to shape their beast-natures into the creatures they wish to become, but have natural tendencies. At the very first, in the womb, it is an unshaped protean form that contains all creatures."

"Perhaps," said Mawa.

"And perhaps not," Lenco added.

Xido had only a weary look for his siblings. "Or not perhaps. I won't debate it." He returned his attention to Qala. "I suspect my son's ability to swim comes from my physical heritage. My human side." A slight snicker from the direction of Mawa. "More or less human. There is no better way to describe it."

"Not from his other nature, then," stated Lura.

"No, not truly. My son will never be a crocodile. Nor, most likely, any other form than that he wears right now."

Qala was glad to hear that. Let that bird or whatever stay inside. But she would definitely like to know more about it! "So Zedos resembles your grandfather, you tell me? His great-grandfather?"

"He does. We know very little of him. I suspect he may even have been a Major Elemental. Were such to bind itself to a form, it would be as a god."

"I have thought this myself," said Lenco. "Maybe all gods are descended from elementals of one sort or another."

Mawa laughed outright. "You know better than to say 'all,' Brother."

Lenco had to chuckle himself. "Of course. An infinite number are descended from elementals."

"And an infinite number are not," Xido finished up. "Which makes it impossible to conclude anything. But yes, Qala, the boy does have a form within him very like that of our grandfather. It was eons ago any of us saw him but we all remember."

"It was in the days of chaos," shivered Mawa. "We ourselves were not yet gods, but as mafadwi. It was our father Krat who shaped our world later."

"And now he, too, has disappeared." All three gods became silent.

"Does it matter?" asked Lura.

"Not so far," Xido replied.

31.

"We are all invited," said Qala. She would not press it but liked the idea of Lura being with her. Ramapee too.

The Cana's smile was not so enigmatic this time. "But no men? Other than the little master."

"Hasala no doubt thinks they are going about important man things this morning."

"Sleepin' late, more likely." That from Damana, who bounced Zedos on her knee as they waited. "They would do well to include Mistress Qala in their important man things!"

Qala was quite inclined to agree. No point in saying so, and it would encourage the girl. Others might not be so tolerant when she expressed opinions.

"Lady?" spoke the girl, somewhat less forcefully. "Could you teach me a little, if it's not too much bother? I mean about weapons, like you have with Ranwif and, um, Horos?"

"Why not have Horos show you?" asked Lura. "You know he would love to." Indeed he would. Qala had noticed.

"I'm afraid of scarin' him off if I ask. Maybe if I — well, knew a little first he would take me seriously. I mean, see me as a comrade in arms rather than a girl."

Both older women had to laugh. "Best he see you as a girl," stated Lura. "Every heroic boy needs a girl to rescue."

"And why shouldn't an heroic girl rescue a boy?" came Qala's retort. "I've done it myself on occasion."

"But you would rather rescue girls, would you not?" asked Damana. "The Lady Galana."

Qala did not feel any of the dynamic between them the young woman's words suggested, did she? This quest was a duty, a duty to a friend. Nothing more. This she must admit to herself. To Damana she replied, chuckling, "A bit old to call a girl maybe. Are we ready?"

"I am," stated the Cana, rising. "Come with us, Ramapee." The priestess had sat wordlessly through all their conversation.

To the wide stone stairs they went, and down to the ground floor. The apartments they sought were to their right. The last time Qala had been here, only Flawum lived in them.

If his family continued to grow, he might need more rooms! But would he even continue to reside here, hidden away in the hills, when he was recognized as celos? It would make sense to move his capital south, closer to the sea.

They were expected and ushered in. "In the nursery, my ladies," said the maid in heavily accented Muram. Two years ago, that language had been frowned upon within the walls of the keep. Sharshic only.

And, too, that was the native tongue of most who lived here, as it was among the peasants of Qala's own estate. She had become passably fluent in it. But she and Hasala had conversed in Muram when last she visited. All nobles knew the language.

The place hadn't changed much. Long before Hasala had wed the king she had been looking after him. The rooms had already felt her touch. The nursery. The same room where Flawum had kept the kidnapped Zedos. The same room where Mawa had substituted a mafadwi changeling — Mong — for the baby and set events moving in a most unexpected direction. Both she and Flawum had ended up in the world of the gods.

Hasala did not look that pregnant. Qala could not guess how far along she might be. She doesn't show it like me or Samee, she thought. She's built thicker in the first place.

"I welcome you all," said the future Queen of Arlacana. "Priestesses, are you not?" she asked, seeing the red robes. "Of Kamat. I recognize that. I would ask your blessings on the little ones."

"And the little one to come," spoke Ramapee. She proceeded to proclaim something in Ildin, surely the asked-for blessing. Hasala seemed slightly surprised that the younger woman had taken the lead on this.

Not so Qala. Lura might be the leader of her people and a powerful sorceress, but her priesthood seemed only a matter of convenience. She would leave most of its duties to others.

Zedos was focused on the two babies asleep in their crib. The twin daughters of Hasala and Flawum, about a year old now. "Jong sisters," he stated, and disappeared. The expected gasp came from the noble-woman; her maid gave a little yelp of mingled fear and surprise.

Qala suspected what would come next. "Do not fear if strange things happen, your highness. None of it will harm you."

"I knew this room was haunted, my lady," hissed the maid, speaking now in Sharshic. "Strange things happened here when —" She glared at Qala. "When *she* was here!"

True enough. "I think he has gone to fetch their sister," Qala said, with a nod toward the little girls.

"Sister? They have a sister?" Shock was turning into something a tad more dangerous — for Flawum.

"Your husband was forced to spend the night with a, um, demon when he disappeared two years ago." No need to tell her it was three demons, was there?

"Oh." The woman regained her composure. "He would never speak of that. Is — is your little boy safe?"

"He should be. What lovely girls," she said, moving closer to the crib and hoping to change the course of their conversation. At least for a little while. "What are their names, my lady?"

Hasala came to stand beside her. "This one is, mmm, yes, Esefala. It's easy to mistake one twin for the other. Even for their mother! And this is Mawena."

"Named for goddesses," remarked Lura.

"Yes, but I do not know who this Mawa is. My husband insisted on it. On both of them, saying they were important to him."

Qala did not think she would explain why. Not that it would hurt anything, but that was for Flawum to decide. "A Baxac goddess," was as far as she was willing to go. "A patroness of childbirth, among other things."

Hasala gave a distracted nod. Her daughters were waking, one fussing, the other crying.

"Sisters," announced Zedos, reappearing with both Jong and Mong. The maid bolted from the room this time.

"Little," was Mong's only comment.

121

"They are young, deary," Damana told him. She looked questioningly at the not-so-little Jong.

"Jong should be three or four months older, I think," said Qala. "Oh, your highness, may I present Jong and Mong?"

Lady Hasala took in Mong's horns without comment. Her eyes lingered on Jong somewhat longer. "Yes, I can see Flawum in her. Welcome to both of you."

"Mong would be her half-brother," explained Qala. "In his mind, I think that makes your girls his sisters too."

Mawena was sitting up, examining this new sister. "Awa ga?" she asked. In response, Jong sang. It was a song without words, but filled with the awful beauty of her home. Maybe there were the calls of birds in it, the rushing of waterfalls in the impossibly high mountains and of wind in depthless chasms. It held the light of a great golden sun and of two silvered moons, and the shadows of secluded secret groves. It yearned for all that was and might be.

Had Qala heard that song, faintly, distantly, in the world of the gods? She realized they all stood there still, entranced, after the little one was finished. She realized there were tears in her eyes.

A noise out in the reception room, someone hurrying, running even. A moment later, Xido burst into the room, a startled guardsman in his wake. He stood staring at those gathered. "Jong?" he choked out. "Was it Jong who sang?"

Lura was the one able to answer. "It was. Do you know that song?"

"It was the melody Krat played on his flute to create a world. She is more powerful than ever we imagined." He slowly shook his head. "Its music called to me, even from a distance."

"It was very beautiful," murmured Damana. "I thought I might have heard it once." The girl suddenly began to sob. "So beautiful it hurts."

"It is woven into every part of our world. You would have felt it when you visited." He paused, pondered briefly. "I suspect our host sensed something of it too. It would be best if I took these youngsters home at once — and spoke to my siblings of this."

"Go too?" asked Zedos.

"No, my son. You must stay and take care of your mother. Here, you

122

two," he called to the little mafadwi. A few seconds later all three disappeared into a cloud of shadow.

"I never realized," remarked Hasala, "my husband had such interesting friends. Who's for lunch?"

32.

"There are Mura who may be just as determined to disrupt our negotiations," stated Corad. "And they would not balk at targeting you, your highness."

The king nodded. "We knew there were opponents on both sides of the border. What we did not anticipate were those who took Lord Vullum's wife." Vullum and Murgom were notably absent. Perhaps Flawum also felt the need to escape them from time to time. "Pirates and smugglers. Working together?"

"At least to the same purpose."

"Hmm, yes. And Lady Qala knows much of these people." Flawum turned his attention to the Muram woman. "I thought Lord Xido would be with you."

"He had to leave." Flawum would be able to guess where he went.

"I had a strange dream — a daydream, perhaps — earlier. I would have liked to discuss it with him."

"That may be related to the reason for his departure. But best not to think too much on such things, your majesty."

"Your majesty? You had no problem addressing me as Flawum once. And manhandling me a bit too."

"You needed and deserved it. Now you deserve to be called 'your majesty.'" It was true. Flawum could still be silly but his time in the world of Krat had changed him. Changed him thoroughly.

"The question now," spoke Corad, attempting to turn the meeting back to its business, "is what do we do about these people, whoever they are, who have kidnapped my mother-in-law?"

"You could send Lord Vullum home," suggested Nedos. "Maybe that would be enough to get her sent back."

Both king and envoy shook their heads. "They will not release her as long as these negotiations go on. Of this I am certain," said Flawum.

To which Corad added, "And if they are concluded successfully, maybe never."

That was possible. Men could be vindictive. Qala chose not to say that. "More likely they would demand some ransom," she said. Which was indeed true. It was what she would have done with a wealthy captive.

She spoke no more but turned her attention to her goblet. The same disappointing vintage this king had served last night. The others sat in silence a few moments.

"We should attempt to retrieve the Lady Galana somehow," said Flawum. "Qala, you do not serve me. I can order you to do nothing. But I ask you, as a friend, to go south and see what you can do."

This had been coming. She had known it. "As a friend, I shall, and as a friend of Galana. But I have no idea what I can do." Even if Xido reappeared and helped her.

"At least you have more knowledge than the rest of us," spoke Corad. "I, uh, might be able to come with you. That depends on Murgom and Vullum, and whether they feel they need me here."

"I need you here, as the voice of common sense." Flawum was quite emphatic. "Do not leave me to those two!"

"But I can accompany Lady Qala," said Nedos. "It is time I returned to my ship."

"You would be welcome, sir," she said. "As would be your own knowledge." The captain gave her a little bow of the head in acknowlededgment.

"And I shall send Ranwif, if he is willing," decided the king.

"Remember, sir," said Qala, "young Ranwif still serves me, not you." She spoke this lightly, almost as banter. It was truth, none the less.

"Quite so, my lady." Flawum raised his cup to her. "But I do expect that to change."

"As do I." She raised her cup as well. "To Ranwif's future." Qala drank and replaced the goblet on the marble-topped table before adding, "As a noble of Arlacana?"

"That is entirely possible, my lady." The Sharshite took a moment to compose himself and his thoughts before going on. "One article of our agreement — our tentative agreement — calls for the abolishing of all traditional Sharshite titles within my realm. Just as I am no longer to be named Ri, so must my nobles relinquish their claims to Mor or Tiarna, and become barons or thegns or the like."

"That seems no great hardship," observed Nedos.

"Yet there are those who will object. Ranwif, should he choose my service, I shall name a knight at once. After all, he already holds the equivalent Muram rank."

"An equester," said Corad. "I bestowed it on him myself." Lord Hurrum should have, but Ranwif objected rather strongly. He would never forgive Corad's father for what he saw as treachery and Hurrum saw as good sense.

"Then, in a little while, a lord." A noble title — but not an hereditary one. It would not yet be time to give those to men, to award estates, with the kingdom newly reborn. "And as a noble, I can appoint him to any sort of important post." Flawum gave them a conspiratorial smile. "How does 'Marshal of the North' sound? I'll need to give someone the responsibility of bringing the wilderness under control and dealing with the Muram border — someone in charge of pretty much everything north of these hills."

Corad considered this. "A large responsibility for a young man," he drawled.

"Which is why it would not be at once. Smaller responsibilities first, such as joining Qala's mission."

"And I shall be glad of his presence." A few extra fighting men might be handy as well. She wouldn't bring that up here. Ranwif would be the one to talk to about arranging it. "Chances are the Cana will want to come along. The south was always her destination."

"Extra cover for us," said Nedos.

Qala agreed. "Quite true. I suspect you Sharshites will want your naps now, having filled your bellies with lunch."

"It is the civilized way to live, my lady," Corad told her. "Perhaps we should take our leave now, your highness, and give you and the Lady Hasala your privacy."

"Is your wife in the nursery?" asked Qala. "I would say my farewell to her." Maybe for some time. She hoped to be off soon — even as early as the morrow, if possible.

"Out with the girls. She said they all needed fresh air. And —"

Flawum halted, uncertain for a moment. "And she gave me the most odd look this morning after your visit."

"I am not surprised, your majesty."

33.

"There are many descendants of Im among these Ildin. He has lived a very long time, after all."

"That is certainly so," agreed Lura. "I would assume you have left a few descendants yourself."

"I am careful of such things," Xido replied. The god had rejoined them as they journeyed forth from Flawum's keep this morning. Qala had anticipated his eventual arrival and made sure they brought along a horse for him.

"Too careful, maybe," sniffed the Cana.

"It would not have done to give you a child. You know this."

She sighed. "I suppose. It is long since I have been in this part of the world."

Qala had never been here. She had visited the coasts to the south and, of course, Flawum's keep, but not the lands between. The vegetation was scrubbier on this side of the hills, more pines rising from the sandy soil and small palms beginning to appear here and there as undergrowth. Those were common down along the Lesser Sea.

Xido was going to tell her nothing unless she asked. So she did. "What thinks your family of Jong?"

"Mawa and Lenco are intrigued and wish to see what happens next. Budo thinks maybe she should be destroyed."

"You spoke to no others?" asked Lura.

"No others are interested. Even if they were, we four are the most powerful. We rule our world." His smile mocked his words. "As much as any do."

Qala had to say, "I can't believe that of Budo."

"He can be as ruthless as any of us. And he is an earnest sort, which makes it all the worse. Budo would be inclined to do what he feels is needed."

They rode on in silence a little while, Qala brooding on this informa-tion. She liked big Budo, trusted him more than his siblings. She hated to think of him so.

"Fear not for little Jong, my Qala. Budo said only 'maybe,'" spoke Xido. He turned to Lura suddenly, riding on his other side. "I just thought of something. You saw Jong. Did you see more, as with Zedos?"

"Her two natures? No, no more than I could her brother's. One is not hidden inside the other as with your son, but mingled."

"So she is as we see her — unless she learns to separate them."

"That would make her a god, would it not? Along with her ability to travel among the universes."

Xido chose not to answer.

At each village they passed, the party stopped long enough for the Cana to speak to the inhabitants in Ildin. Most here were of that people; few Sharshites had ever migrated this far south. At the coast it would be different. Sharshite and Muram and Baxac folk mingled there in the ports. Ildin too, to be sure.

Qala couldn't follow the language well but understood she was inviting them to join her on the journey across the mountains to a new home. Some might go. Some already had, she knew, traveling around this southern end of the range to enter the Veltar's lower valley. Lura hoped to establish her people's haven further north, away from the coast.

Hadn't Marana told her that Sharshites were also crossing into this new land? Outcasts, escaped slaves, bandits — disaffected folk of all sorts, hoping to escape the oppressive rule of the Muram Empire. That was much further north, through other ways than the pass near the Cana's home. Who might guess what sort of world all these people might create over there, given a few centuries? She certainly wouldn't see it. Xido would, were he interested enough to look in.

Right now, Xido needed to look in on the situation with Galana again. Maybe Saj had seen more. Maybe this wizard he mentioned knew something. Lura could speak with them at a distance, could she not? Ah, but it was days to the coast where the kidnapped woman was held. Probably held. There was no point in being impatient.

They rode on through that first day, and camped beside a substantial Ildin village. The Ildin here, as everywhere, were a hospitable people and welcomed them. "Lura's grandfather traveled through this land with me, when first he came to this world," Xido told them. "It has not changed so much, though near a thousand years have passed."

"He has told me tales of it," said Lura. "I suspect he exaggerated some of them."

"Most likely. Still, he was very young and rather foolish, and inclined to get himself into difficulties." He winked at her. "And there were young and foolish Ildin women to help him with that."

"I think maybe you exaggerate now."

"Xido's tales always grow over the years," said Lenco, stepping out of the darkness beyond their campfire.

"You are alone?" asked his brother.

"Mawa is curious about the little mafadwi girl and is investigating. She certainly is not going to leave that up to Budo." The god took a seat among the others there. "Any supper left?"

"All devoured, I am afraid," said Nedos, "but we've a skinfull of wine." He passed it to Lenco who tipped it up and drank its stream expertly, spilling not a drop.

Xido ignored his brother. "I still await your story, Captain Nedos. You've promised it but events keep getting in the way of its telling."

"It's our fault for living interesting lives," responded the sailor. "Where to begin? With Marana and Saj arriving in Lorj? I took them there on my ship, you know."

"We do," said Qala. "They wrote to Corad about all that but their letters grew more vague later."

"Well, they took the Imperial Road south and had some adventures. Met this Im for the first time and he sort of took them under his wing, to hear Marana tell it. They say he had some kind of monster that followed him about?" Nedos sounded at least slightly skeptical of this.

"Indeed he did," spoke Lura. "A demon."

"Hmm, it's a good thing, I reckon, because they were attacked by one of those snake-things you fought, Xido. A bakawan. But this one was only about half the size."

Xido nodded. "Yes, the bakawan. I remember. I took on my crocodile form to contest with it." He shrugged. "After that, I can recall very little."

"It goes with who we are, my brother," commented Lenco. "The bakawan is a creature from the world of the Kohari gods. The spawn of Bagap, they call it."

"Bagap is a god, isn't he?" asked Qala. "I've heard the name in southern ports."

"A god of the Kohari. And, like us, dispossessed of many worshipers by the cult of Munu."

Nedos chuckled. "Ah, but the priests of Munu sent the bakawan after Saj. Twice!"

"It is only a rather brainless beast. Anyone could command it," said Xido. "And it is not really the spawn of Bagap, though I think it might have been bred by him."

"Possibly. I have visited Bagap, serpent to serpent," claimed Lenco. "As most serpent gods, he is also a god of male sexuality. But he is far too protean to have much in common with a little god such as I. He is all about the creation of his world, and life and death and all of that."

"A chaos god," Xido added. "It is his wife who gave their world form."

Lenco laughed. "So she claims! I don't trust any goddess who is served by headhunters."

"Enough of these digressions," scolded Lura. "I want to hear this tale before we sleep. Do go on, Captain Nedos."

He did, as the fire slowly burnt down.

34.

Nedos seemed to be wrapping up his story at last. "And so they wandered about in the mountains and took turns being kidnapped. In the process, they picked up the priestess Kataree."

"Priestess of what god?" asked the Cana.

"Of Asak, then." The god of evil. Nedos paused to allow that to make an impression. "Now she serves the goddess Arimanata. When she doesn't serve me." The captain grinned broadly.

"Kamat's wife. A definite improvement."

"I like to think I am too. Anyway, when I came upon them they had been captured again, this time by the very pirates I was pursuing. Im was there too but his, um, demon had apparently died a short time before. I never saw it."

"Akorzef," murmured Xido. "Or so I knew it. Im had taken to calling it Cory."

"According to this Im and another wizard that seemed to be playing both sides — what was his name? Nanos, that's it. According to them these pirates had been sent by their king especially to nab them and some jewels they had. And he was working with a sorcerer far away, Joker or something like that."

"Dxukur?" asked Lura.

"Could be."

"The current Wizard-Lord," observed Xido. "There is more going on than we realized."

"There is always more going on than we realize," said Nedos. "I learned that a long time ago. Pass me that wine skin, will you? Story-telling is thirsty work."

Once refreshed, he continued. "Kataree and I hit it off right away. Which is why she is now my wife. I count myself deucedly lucky that the right woman came along at the right time! My boys and I escorted them up to the coast where we had captured the pirates' ship, and prepared to sail on to Matanas with our prize."

"But more was going on than you realized," came Lenco's dry comment.

"Indeed so. Seems the Pirate King had wind of us, thanks to his wizard maybe, and sent a fleet. Saj and Kataree fought it off with every magic trick they could think of but we were sure to be overtaken before we made it to safety. Then —" He fixed his eyes on Xido. "Then a huge crocodile popped up out of nowhere and began banging their ships about. We made our escape and that was that."

The god nodded slowly. "So that is how I saved Saj twice, is it? I must have awakened right after that and returned to our world."

"It's the sort of thing that might do it," agreed Lenco. "As long as you peacefully cruised the oceans you would have been content to remain a mindless crocodile."

"I am fairly sure that Saj called me somehow. Possibly with those jewels you mentioned, Captain."

"Don't know anything about them. Never even saw them either! Saj did take home a full set of carpentry tools from the pirate ship I captured. I suspect he took something more from it, for both he and my bride-to-be suddenly had a great deal of money they would not explain. I did not press, for we used some of that to buy the captured galley at auction at Matanas." His smile spoke of satisfaction. "Kataree is very much my business partner as well as my wife.

"But Saj — between the tools and the money he quickly got a thriving construction business going in Lanlaz, and soon had a finger in just about everything. And he seems to always know just what endeavor might succeed or fail."

"His second sight," said Qala.

"Indeed. Kataree knows all about it, as she has gifts of her own."

The Cana rose from her place by the fire. "I should try to speak with her. Not tonight. It is already late and we all need rest."

Qala was surprised her son was still awake. Zedos had appeared to pay attention through Nedos's account. That he understood much of it, she doubted. "We need to get you to bed too," she told him.

The answer was a quite emphatic, "No."

Damana tried not to look amused. "No has been his favorite word of late, my lady," she said.

Qala sighed. "Maybe I should let his father take charge of him for a while."

"I fear he would spoil the boy somethin' terrible. Do we keep goin' south tomorrow?"

"More or less. I think we turn westerly some, toward the river."

The girl nodded, though it might have meant nothing to her. She might not even know what river it was. "Samee came from around here." Qala was not sure if it was a question or a statement.

"I suppose. Hmm, no, probably further north, back in the hills." Where the folk were at least partially Sharshite, culturally.

"Oh." Damana giggled. "I don't think the little master will say 'no' again." Zedos had gone quite to sleep. "I'll get him settled down. And myself!" She carried the boy off to his blankets, and lay herself down beside him. In a minute or two, she slumbered as well.

But Qala did not feel like sleeping. Some had gone to their rest; others remained yet about the dying fire. She returned to sit with them, taking a place beside Ramapee. Where was Horos? Oh, there, conferring with the Cana's men. Setting sentries, she guessed.

It was just as well Ranwif left it to the boy, though Qala herself should be in charge here and apportion duties. Maybe she would assert herself tomorrow. "Have you ever traveled south before?" she asked the young woman at her side.

"No, my lady. I was born and grew up in the sacred valley. Mec Lura has dragged me across the mountains a couple times lately, but never this direction."

Qala stretched out her legs, moving her feet closer to the embers. Even this far south it could be cool at night — and Qala detested the cold. "A new adventure for both of us, then. I thought I was past the age for them!"

"Oh, no, Lady Qala. You are young still." The girl snickered in a rather unladylike manner. "Now the Cana, she is old."

"Well I know it. And once again, it is Qala, not Lady."

"Yes, Qala."

"Perhaps you shall met a nice young Ildin man down this way."

Ramapee smiled, again almost as enigmatically as her mistress. "I think not."

"Priestesses of Kamat marry, do they not?" Qala had never heard otherwise.

"Some do, some do not." She gave Qala a sidelong look. "As with pirates perhaps."

Of course she would know Qala's past. The Cana was surely knowledgeable and would have confided in her aide. Indeed, the young Ildin pretty much fitted the job description for 'confidante.' Qala only nodded, and sat quietly for a minute or two. Nedos and the gods were speaking of something in low voices. If they wished to share, they would.

"I'm for bed," she said, rising.

35.

It was not to be expected that Lenco would still be there at dawn. With Xido, she thought the odds closer to even and there he was, ready to ride on with them. That made fourteen traveling south, with the pair of Flawum's fighting men Ranwif had added.

Hardly a formidable force. Qala did not believe at all that their enemies had given up, but maybe this group of travelers would not seem to offer any threat to them. They were only riding down to Arlak-Port, not going to see a king nor deliver a message, as before.

She whispered these thoughts to Nedos. Somehow she put more trust in him right now. He knew the coasts better than the others, even better than Xido. "Perhaps so," he replied, and then gave her a long look. "Unless they recognize who you are. This Quso would not want the former ruler of his realm nosing about in pirate affairs."

"You know who I am, then." She had never told the man. Could Corad have let it slip?

"I've put things together. In truth, I had my suspicions when first we pulled you and your friends from the water." She had known that at the time. "Saj and Marana eventually let me in on the rest of it."

"Chances are you know more of the Pirate King and his activities than I do, these days. It is near three years since I was queen." Three? Yes, come autumn. "I have heard he abandoned our old base."

"The pirate enclave is somewhere on the western coast of Lorj now. Certainly safer than lurking near the mouth of the Chas."

"But further from the prizes we, um, they seek. That's like Quso, to prefer caution."

Nedos accepted that insight without comment. "Do you know those coasts, Qala?"

"I sailed many coasts. I did not always remain on the Rock in our hidden base." Ah, she missed sailing before the wind, sailing upon the Great Sea with none to stay her. "I might even be able to guess where the new hiding spot is." But she would not betray her former comrades. Unless it were truly necessary; things did happen, after all. "This road leads us to Arlak-Port?"

"We'll need become accustomed to calling it Arlacas. But, aye, this is the way. We draw near the river by tomorrow and parallel it down to the coast."

The day proved uneventful. And hot, until rain swept in from the south, mid-afternoon. They halted early and found shelter in one of the villages along the way.

"A grain-storage barn," said Xido, looking about the building they had been offered. "In a month or two there might have been not space for us."

"Then let us be glad it is now and not a month or two hence," replied the Cana. "I should attempt to speak to Kataree now. Do you wish to join me, Xido?"

The god shrugged. "I might as well. That won't put us into contact with Saj, though. It's his talent we need."

"We live close," Nedos pointed out. "A day or so by water."

"Very well. Still, it might have been simpler for me to visit him again."

He and Lura took seats on the earthen floor, a bit apart from the others. A moment later, Qala was fairly sure they were elsewhere. "I think maybe you have become as used to this as I," Ramapee whispered to the captain.

"It is part of being married to a sorceress," he replied. "It took a while to convince her to keep it private. People did give her odd looks when she'd go off into a trance in a tavern or the like."

Qala spoke. "I saw Saj go away many a time when he sought within the Eyes." And the aged sorcerer who had served the pirates before him. "That's a bit different though." This last half-sounded like a question, she realized.

"I never saw Mec Lura actually use the Fire Stone," admitted Ramapee. "You were there when all four were reunited?"

A nod. She had no real idea what they were at the time, only that the Sea Stone let a wizard look to what might happen on the wide waters. "They're coming back."

It was no surprise that Xido was the first to return, almost instantly alert. He would forever have the vigor of youth, despite the weight of unnumbered millennia upon him. "Im was unexpected," he said. "It was good to speak with him again. But he is so old." It was almost as if he had difficulty believing it — or did not wish to.

"It happens to all of us, my little god," Lura told him.

Xido sighed deeply, more deeply than Qala ever remembered of him. "He has lasted far longer than most of my mortal friends but, as all of them, he will be lost to me. A century? A millennium? What are these beside eternity?"

The Cana chose not to answer. How could she? "I did not know the other with him."

"Nanos." The god turned his head to Nedos. "You mentioned him, did you not?"

"A rival whom he accepted as an apprentice of sorts," replied the sailor. "Or just as someone to take care of him."

"Entirely possible," said Xido. "He would have missed having a companion, once Cory was gone. The man seemed powerful enough, but not a match to your grandfather, Lura, nor even you."

"Im probably remains the most powerful wizard alive." She gave Zedos, sitting in Horos's lap, a long look. "Your son may well claim Grandfather's title one of these days."

"His talents may lie elsewhere. I wish she could have convinced Saj to join the conversation. He is capable if he wishes. Oh, Captain," he called, "your lovely wife is in Lanlaz with Marana and Saj. She thought it best."

"Or got bored with the little town of Nota," responded Nedos. "As long as she is safe and well, it's all good with me. So she'll be able talk to Saj right off, I take it."

"It is to be hoped. Right now, let us concern ourselves with supper and sleep," spoke Lura. She tipped her head, listening. "I hear no rain on the roof. Perhaps our hosts will feed us and I can speak my message in yet another village."

A plan that appealed to pretty much everyone. As they exited the barn, Qala leaned in and whispered to Damana, "Did you hand my son to young Horos?"

The girl snickered. "It seemed a good way to make him stay put when I sat down beside him."

Her mistress had to admit it was. "Practice for things you have planned?" she asked.

Damana actually blushed. A most rare occurrence! "Maybe, Mistress."

"Be careful. He's a good boy. I have plans of my own for him."

She nodded vigorously. "I'm making sure not to scare him off. I think —" Damana hesitated and maybe even reddened again. "I think he is a virgin."

Though she said it not, Qala thought it likely too. "Who is to say what might come? I can but hope for the best for the both of you, whether together or apart. Ah, a fire! That is welcome."

There was a blaze going in the community firepit, and many Ildin villagers of both sexes and all ages sat by it. "I would hope the same for you, Qala," whispered Damana. "And for Ramapee."

Then she moved away before Qala could ask the girl what she meant.

36.

Sometimes, Ramapee took charge of her son, carrying him before her on her saddle. Qala liked the quiet woman's ways. So, apparently, did Zedos. They had glimpsed the Arlak, off and on through this day, a broad swampy river. Qala knew it was not much different at its mouth, remaining shallow and slow-moving.

A sudden, loud demand. "Halt!" cried out Xido.

Qala held up a hand herself to signal an official stop. Some would look to her for that. As well they should. Ranwif, in the lead, repeated the signal for the whole of the small column of riders.

Lura and Xido were already dismounted. "I would guess Kataree has called," said Ramapee. "Let's get you down, young man, and let you stretch your legs."

"Go pee-pee," he responded as she lifted him to the ground. "Ramapeepee." He laughed at his joke quite loudly.

That was something else new. "That's not very polite," Qala told him.

"Oh." Zedos looked up the Ildin woman. "Sorry — Ramapeepee." He broke into laughter again.

Qala shook her head and took his hand. "Let's get you into the bushes. The way you're laughing you may already have wet yourself."

When she returned with her son, miraculously dry, Xido and Lura were speaking from afar. They took some time about it.

"I have never been within the Jewels before," were the Cana's first words on returning.

"You weren't really now," Xido told her. "Not the way Saj or your grandfather have been."

"Or you. It was good that Saj could use them to show us what he had seen." She frowned. "But I recognized nothing."

"On the coast somewhere, and not too far from us. Between Arlak-Port and Pas I would wager."

"Yes. Not in a large town. That I could see. We should describe the place we saw to Qala and Captain Nedos. They might know it."

"In camp tonight. Let's ride now." Xido mounted his ride. The others followed. There was no reason not do as he said.

Lura and Xido rode side by side; Qala though it was to discuss their vision — or whatever one named it — but no speech passed between them. At last the Cana said, "I see why you and Im felt the Eyes of the Wind should be separated. One who possesses them all could wield great power."

"That power will be needed soon."

"But not by Saj."

"No. He is the caretaker for now, the one who gathered them and will have them ready when the conflict comes. Yet —" A slight smile crossed Xido's homely face. "Saj will make good use of them in the mean time, I believe, preparing his family and his city." He looked back over his shoulder at the woman who rode close behind them. "That may include you, Qala."

"I would appreciate any warnings," she admitted. "None of this is very soon, I understand."

"He told me his sons would be grown before anything happened," said Lura. "That is a fair amount of time to get ready."

I might not even be alive, she told herself, and Zedos will be a man. He could be the one who needed warnings.

"Yes, his sons," agreed Xido. "Saj can not see his own future but saw theirs."

"Some," added Lura.

"Some," he agreed, and rode on.

It was not until evening and a meal that the two felt ready to share their account, taking turns and occasionally interrupting each other. They listened politely until the end. Qala and Nedos exchanged a knowing look.

"You are wrong," Qala told him. Nedos nodded an agreement.

"West of Arlak-Port," he said.

"Right. On the cape. One doesn't see cliffs like that to the east."

"A wreckers village, I would wager." said Nedos. The long cape that jutted out into the Greater Sea beyond the mouth of the Arlak was notorious for shipwrecks. "Or smugglers. They've always found it a good place to hide out."

"True enough. I've done business there myself."

"Very well. At least we know now," Xido stated.

"But it will not be nearly so easy to approach," Nedos told him. "There are no roads, and no good harbors along its length, only small coves suited to rowboats."

"Or a handy little sailboat." The one she had left behind at Melawhem would have done fine. Or a crocodile. Qala would not suggest that.

"We should arrive at Arlak-Port tomorrow," said Nedos. "Not much point to planning more till we're settled in. Remember, I have a ship there."

"But not really suited to the job," Qala observed. "Not easy to keep from being spotted, either."

"I could creep close at night and drop a boat or two. But that is most iffy when we don't know the precise spot."

Qala had said nothing of it but thought she *had* recognized the precise spot. She had more intimate knowledge of the lawless men who dwelt on the cape than Nedos ever might. All this could be revealed later. It was not in her nature to say things before they were needed. "Dangerous waters to ply at night," she commented.

And Captain Nedos had no reason to risk himself or his ship. What cared he for Lady Galana? For that matter, the treaty would not mean that much to him. To be sure, it would present new opportunities for business but an able man would always find those.

Able woman, too, she reminded herself.

There seemed no more to be said so they wandered in various direc- tions, some taking in this substantial village, some walking down to the River Arlak flowing beside it. There were docks here, and boats. Crude boats, by Qala's standards, many of them dugouts. Cypress stood high across the flow, the Arlak disappearing among them.

This town was built on a low bluff and reasonably dry. Despite that, mosquitoes buzzed constantly in Qala's ears. It was to be expected. Arlak-Port was the same — except wetter! All this would become part of Flawum's new kingdom, would it not? He had always claimed it, of course, as had his ancestors, but never controlled it. The Mura paid little attention to the area, mostly concentrating themselves on the coast around Pas, and letting the people live the slow, simple lives of their ancestors.

Lots of flotsam. The summer rainy season would bring that down the river. Well, maybe. For all Qala knew there was always flotsam, branches, logs, leaves, coming down, heading for the sea, not knowing its destination, not caring.

She was hungry. She turned and walked back into the village.

37.

Arlak-Port was not too different from when last she had seen it. Four or five years? There had never been much reason for Qala to come ashore here.

With things about to change — maybe change? No, make that probably change. With things probably about to change, she might need to take more interest. Flawum was friendly to her. He would be willing to grant all sorts of favors when it came to trading in his new port.

The town smelled as bad as ever. It must be low tide, with the mudflats exposed. The shallow flow of the Arlak River, winding through those flats, was an impediment to success as a port. The usable channels changed with some regularity.

On the other hand, it really was a rather well-protected place with the cape to its west, blocking the waves and winds of the Great Sea. Little of importance came from the other direction, where lay numerous islands, including Lorj itself. Only a swell from the southwest need be a concern; that and the great cyclones of summer and fall. Even those rarely caused much trouble here.

"There's my ship," said Nedos, pointing to a slim dark craft in the river. "The *Mursilla*."

Qala cast a questioning look his way. "Named for Kataree's mother. Long deceased."

"It looks like a fighting ship," she observed.

"It was. It's the vessel I captured and then bought. It's small, admittedly, and not that suited to cargo, but it sails fast."

She shielded her eyes from the sun, one hand above, the other below to block the glare on the water. "You've removed the rowers' stations. Most of them."

"Can't afford men at the oars. I added some to the sails. See the new sail at the back?"

It was one of the triangular shape that was catching on. Qala knew from experience they worked well on small boats.

"So what do you carry? Or is it just for personal amusement, Captain Nedos?"

"Mostly I use it for human cargo."

"Slaves?"

"No, no, my lady!" The captain was choking with laughter. "Passengers. Men and women who want swift passage up and down the coast."

"Oh. Of course." Like many Sharshites, Nedos likely took a dim view of slavery. Qala had thought it a necessary evil, once. Not so much now — perhaps she was turning into more of a Sharshite than she realized.

But the holding of slaves had not always the large scale it had taken on in the empire. Agricultural slavery was unheard of in the Old Kingdoms, nor was it common in the imperial homeland, that cold rocky land lying well north of Sharsh. The freeholders there would never have permitted it. Saj's people.

Still, someone had to row galleys. By now they were in the town, riding up a mud-encrusted cobblestone pavement. It would be a stretch to call it a city, though it was trying its best. "I do not think I can put you all up on my ship," announced Nedos. "But if you think you would prefer to sleep on my decks you are welcome."

"The mosquitoes will be dreadful in the open," Qala warned them.

"Sandflies, too," added the sailor. She had forgotten them. They were even worse. You couldn't hear them coming.

Nor see them. "Maybe we should search out an inn," she suggested. One with room for a dozen. Twelve and a half, including Zedos. Nedos offered no suggestions, bidding them farewell, dismounting and strolling on toward his waiting ship, a sack across his shoulder.

"Let us seek in that direction," spoke Lura, pointing eastward. "Ildin men and women coming from the countryside would frequent such places, on the outskirts of the town."

"Rather than sailors and ne'er-do-wells from the docks," said Xido.

More his sort, thought Qala. Perhaps mine too. At times, at times. She had frequented many a dive in her early days and come out none the worse for it. Some of those who encountered her had not fared so well. They turned on what appeared a major way. Possibly the road to Pas. What other important road would enter from the east? There was more traffic than she expected. Maybe this place was waking up to its future.

Xido gestured toward a compound to their left. It looked clean enough but — no rooms? Only sheds for travelers to camp with their

145

goods and their animals, sheds with straw for bedding. Lura nodded. "Looks good enough," Qala added to this. No one else's thoughts mattered much, and all recognized this.

She left it to the Cana and the deity to dicker with their landlord. It was all in Ildin. "The mosquitoes will still be bad," she mentioned at the conclusion.

"But better than by the river," said Xido. "And we may avoid other pests as well."

"Men who serve Quso. Spies."

"Spies to be sure. Worse too, maybe. They did try to kill us on the road, after all. They may try to kill us here."

Ranwif stood near, holding his mount's reins, surrounded by his men. "We'll mount a guard, as we have all along. Horos first watch, me second, Augun last."

"Thank you, sir," spoke Augun, chuckling. Some did not understand the cause of that but Qala knew the former pirate was always an early riser anyway. Smart of Ranwif to recognize that. And good of him to take the middle watch.

The three sorted out which of their men would sit each watch, while Qala led the horses into their stable. She was not about to leave hers to someone else to tend, not on a journey such as this. Each must pull her or his weight. To their credit, all did, the Cana included.

The Cana, Mec Lura — would she remain with them now or travel eastward, spreading her news to more of her people? She would miss Ramapee's presence. Ah, people came, people went. This would end and she would return home with her son. That was what mattered. Qala drifted into sleep, but tossed fitfully through the night. Once she thought she felt Zedos's small hand on her arm, his voice whispering, "Sleep, Mommy." But it was dream, wasn't it?

When she woke again, Augun was leading the watch. She might as well get up herself. No, she was still tired. Her muscles ached. Who was that talking with Augun, over by the stable? Not one of their people. A groom maybe but he didn't have the look.

More likely a sailor by his clothes. Qala felt herself falling asleep again. In the morning, she was not sure whether she had dreamed this too.

38.

"I am still not sure I trust the man," stated Xido.

"I've no reason not to," she said. Except for that odd dream last night, if that was what it was.

No, she would rather have Augun guarding her than any man. Even Ranwif. She trusted the seasoned pirate's judgment when danger threatened. More so in the streets of a town such as this. "And I count myself as good a sword arm as any."

"Better, I would say. So be it; I am hardly the one to prohibit you from anything."

It was no great matter anyway. She only meant to walk down to the harbor and speak with Nedos. There were things they knew better than these others. They were the ones who should hash out some start to a plan. And maybe she could look at boats while at it. A small sailing vessel seemed almost a necessity to her, after turning things over in her head for a while.

"Go," said Zedos. "Not stay with Damana." The boy turned a disapproving eye to the girl, talking to Horos. Now and then, Horos actually talked back.

"But I would have to bring Damana along if you came," she explained.

"Ramapee. Go with Ramapee."

"Hmm, well I suppose if she would be willing to come in Damana's stead. Ramapee," she called, "would you like to walk to the harbor with us?"

The young woman consented without the slightest moment of hesitation.

"You shall to carry this lump of a boy at times," Qala warned. "And I might stop in at some tavern or shop to check the wind blowing through Arlak-Port. You lead, Augun."

"Bye-bye," called Zedos from Ramapee's arms and then sticking out his tongue at his erstwhile nursemaid. Qala suspected the girl did not at all mind a free hour or two.

"Are you trying to make Damana jealous, young man?" asked the Ildin. "That is no way for a gentleman to act."

"Oh. Alright." The boy seemed unusually thoughtful for a few seconds. "Wrong hurt Horos?"

"Very wrong," his mother assured him. She was momentarily taken aback by the thought that her little demigod son just might be able to harm the boy. His powers would only increase, too.

"Marry Damana."

"You?" asked Ramapee.

The boy laughed at the idea. "No, 'tupid-head. Horos."

"It might happen," admitted the girl. "So who will you marry?"

"Watch your language, my boy," added Qala.

He looked into her face. "Not Ramapee. Mommy marry."

"You can't marry your mommy."

Zedos looked quite exasperated. He might even have considered calling her a stupid-head again. "No. Mommy marry *you*."

The woman immediately colored to a shade of red Qala did not think possible for a human. Was there something there? Was this young Ildin lady attracted to her — or more than attracted? She would have to sort that out later, as well as her own feelings. Those were just as difficult to get a grasp on.

"Let's stop in here for a bite and a drink," she said, ducking into the nearest wine-shop.

"And something for Zedos to chew on," added Ramapee. "I noticed he is teething again."

"Grogodile teeef!" crowed the boy. "Tomp-tomp!"

Qala had no idea whether her son's teething followed a normal human schedule. The barkeep was entirely willing to give him a chunk of hard-tack to chew while the women sipped an execrable brownish wine. He was a wizened old man, one Qala was sure she had never set eyes on before. Nor he on her, she hoped.

"Jov and Esefa!" said the man. "He's crunchin' it like a dog with his bone."

"That he is," agreed Qala. "I hear there are to be big changes in this town."

"Won't change nothin' for me. I sell wine and people drink it. That's all that matters." He leaned in close to the women. Qala allowed it,

148

despite his odor. "I'm hopin' that certain parties put a stop to all this change."

"I have heard that certain merchants are opposed to it," commented Ramapee, giving a fairly convincing show of enjoying her wine. It was really enough that she did not gag.

The old man nodded vigorously, the scraps of white hair on his scalp flying back and forth. "That tale be true, m'lady. I've heard that some of the Pretender's flunkies rode in yesterday. They'd better think twice about takin' over down here!"

Qala paid their tab and a bit more, though neither had drank more than half her order. "Nothing useful from him," she remarked as they exited through the open door. "No information, just rumor. We'll try another shop later. Closer to the harbor."

"Are you sure you won't be recognized?"

That was her one concern. No one here would have seen her in the last three years or longer, but one could not rely on that. "I doubt it," was what she said.

Augun had waited in the street. He now took up the lead again. "There's an alley down here, Qala, that takes you to the water direct. Remember?"

Qala did not. Augun was likely to know the town better than she did. "Let's use it." She suddenly wanted to get to Nedos and his ship, get things moving."

It was a narrow way between frame buildings, two or three stories mostly, and all shabby and gray. Nor were there stones beneath the feet here, only soft and somewhat damp sand. But she could see the river at its far end.

In a block, then another. It was quieter here than she would have expected. A man stepped out before them, and other men arrayed behind him. She could hear men moving into position at her back. There was no reason to look at them.

"Quso?" gasped Augun.

It was Quso indeed, a rather nondescript fellow with a bit of a pot, and about as Muram looking as it was possible to look. His hair was black where it still grew. "Augun. Come to see your old captain?"

Was Augun truly a traitor? Had he led them into a trap? The burly Mur spat. "I'd rather sail with any other man alive," he rasped out. "Or woman."

That was good to hear, though it was but a very slight improvement of their odds. "What do you want, Quso?" she asked. "I'm not in the business anymore."

"No, only trying to destroy mine," answered the Pirate King. "I would reckon you're hoping to rescue that Sharshite floozy." He drew out his cutlass. "Killing you would send a much clearer message to your little king. And I would greatly enjoy it."

Quso could not have matched her with a sword on his best day and her worst. Therefor, he would leave it to his men. Qala's own blade was in her hand as she stood shoulder to shoulder with Augun. "Get back against the wall," she commanded Ramapee. "Keep my son out of the way."

The pirate leader held up a hand, signaling his men to halt their advance. "Son?" He looked from Qala to the woman holding her child. "So much better! You will not die today, my lady. Another hostage is just the thing to turn you to our cause." He motioned his men forward. "Take the child."

Augun charged forward, recklessly, knocking one man down, wounding another. He is trying to help me escape, Qala realized. She turned toward the men behind her, attacking without hesitation. No, she could not break through. She was pushed back to the wall, Ramapee and Zedos behind her. Augun lay on the ground.

"No!" yelled Zedos, only once and very loud. He reached out a hand to his mother.

A sudden feeling of vertigo, a feeling Qala recognized. A moment later, the three of them were in another world.

Part IV.
ESEFA'S PROMISE

39.

"I am pretty sure this is the valley of Krat. Is Ir's cave near here, Zedos?"

Her son pointed to the golden, sun-drenched cliffs rising above the too-green, too-lush jungle. All was too-something here, the flowers too-red or too-white, the sky too-blue. The world too-beautiful and too-awful.

"I feel small here," spoke Ramapee. "Is it dangerous?"

Qala was not sure. She had seen no wild beasts, been threatened by no mafadwi, when last she was here. But she was in the company of gods then. "Let's get out of the open as soon as we can." She thought she remembered the way.

Yes, here was the stone-lined path she had trod, near two years since. Close up, shadows revealed the cliffs as a darker, ruddy sandstone. Where was the fissure leading into Ir's den?

"Mong!" called out Zedos. There the little mafadwi was, and other small figures with him.

Ramapee giggled, albeit a tad nervously. "The neighborhood children."

Exactly so. Young mafadwi at play. Three? No, four. There was little Jong, a bit apart. It must be safe enough here if their mothers let them out.

Why, these were the children Flawum fathered here, all but Mong of the same age. He *was* bigger than the others. Aside from Jong, they were boys.

Two of those immediately darted into the cave, its entrance easily visible now. "Scared 'em," stated Zedos.

Mong nodded in agreement. "Thithies."

"They are younger than you. Just babies," Qala told them.

"Babieth." Mong liked that. "Babieth, babieth, babieth. Jong baby too."

"Jong brave baby," commented Zedos. Qala decided not to point out that she knew them already. Her anyway.

Ir appeared at the cave door, brandishing an astonishingly large cudgel. The two little ones peeked from behind her muscular legs. "Qala," she said, lowering her club. "Welcome always in cave of Ir!" The mafadwi turned to Zedos. "You bring visit more now and then."

"Yes, Milk-mommy."

"Come in cave. Ir make tea! Oh-oh. God coming."

Qala followed the mafadwi's eyes, to spy a dark young woman coming up the path. It was no god she had seen before but she doubted not her deity. Not a moment.

"Lutanawa!"

"That's Lady Lutanawa, my fine mafadwi," she spoke in haughty tones, before breaking down into laughter. "It has been long, Ir."

"You come visit more now and then too."

"I'll try." She looked down at little Zedos. He looked up at her. "My cousin. The son of Xido, right?"

Qala only nodded. "I have felt the boy's comings and goings this past year."

They followed the goddess into Ir's cave. "Cousin, my lady?" asked Qala.

"Ages ago Lenco gave a child to a human woman of this world. I, Lutanawa, am that child. My mother has long faded into the dust of the past but I have proved immortal."

"Then you are a god."

"That's the consensus. And I turn into a snake, just like Dad." She grinned wickedly. "Except I am poisonous."

Whether this goddess resembled her father or even the rest of her family, Qala was not certain. She was not as sleek as Mawa, more rugged and muscular, yet more attractive in the ways most counted important.

"Play here," Ir ordered the assembled mafadwi children. The two little boys of Jong's age seemed more advanced physically, darting about where she still waddled a bit. Their babysitter busied herself at the fire, apparently in preparation for the making of tea.

Lutanawa whispered, "Ir won't serve you anything dangerous to humans. That does not mean it will taste good."

"Thank you for letting us know, my lady," whispered Ramapee in reply.

"Looty. Call me Looty. I would have you as my friend. Both of you." She might have said it to both but her eyes were on the Ildin woman. Qala did not think she liked that.

But not her concern, as long as Ramapee was not placed in danger here. She was her responsibility.

"Good moss tea," announced Ir, dumping an unappealing mass of tangled gray-green into a crock. "Let steep now."

"I suspect some of your relatives will show up soon," commented Qala. "If only Xido. He would know we were missing."

The goddess shrugged. "I could take you back right now if you wish. Hmm, maybe not Zedos. He has his own will and his own powers."

"Or you could go tell him?" wondered Ramapee.

"Oh, it's more fun to let them figure it out themselves." She gazed a while at Zedos. "Yes, he has power but he is mortal. I can feel this. He will grow old and disappear. I once had a son with a human and he was so. Nothing hurts more than to watch your child age when you can not."

"Perhaps," suggested Ramapee, "it is as bad to watch your parents age and die."

"I have seen both. It is a terrible thing to be mortal."

"As it is to be immortal," said Qala.

Lutanawa nodded. "That too."

"Introduce us to your friends," said Ramapee of a sudden, addressing Zedos. "It is good manners."

"All of them," added Lutanawa. "I've never met them."

The boy put an arm around his best friend. "Mong. Milk-brother!"

The mafadwi revealed many sharp teeth with his broad smile. "Jong. Mong sister." He only casually waved an arm her direction.

"The three little ones have some different heritage, don't they?" spoke Lutanawa, low. "I can feel it."

153

"Their father is mortal," Qala told her, "but with heritage from gods. The Sharshite Ancients."

"Oh. That certainly explains the girl's look. She is going to be big!"

"Gam-gam," announced Zedos, putting his hand on one of the boy's two heads. The child looked somewhat human, in most other respects. "And Gok." The little mafadwi seemed timid. For a moment, Qala thought he was leaving them, fading as a god might, but then realized he was changing color to match the floor of the cave.

"He looks the most like a mortal," observed Lutanawa. "I suspect he could pass as one."

"If he can maintain the proper color," Qala said.

"And all mortal, in the mafadwi sense. Which means very long-lived. All except the girl." She looked at the child quite some time. "I think she is a goddess."

"Tea ready!" called Ir.

40.

Qala was a little disappointed it did not taste worse. Rather bland, rather flavorless, actually. But one needed avoid breathing in the aroma, which reminded her of dank, long-closed rooms.

Nerua and Dem-dem, mothers respectively of Gok and Gam-gam, collected their children and left again. On her previous visit, Qala had assumed all three female mafadwi lived in this cave. They were not at all talkative. Blame that on Lutanawa's presence, she told herself. The mafadwi seemed afraid of her and maybe she should be too. Yet Ir did not seem intimidated.

Ir was one of the most powerful of her kind. Enough hints had been dropped by Zedos's relatives for her to figure that out. She might be closer to those gods' own ancestors.

That was no importance to her. She sat and mostly listened as the other three gossiped. She wouldn't have thought it of Ramapee, that she could settle so readily. Her eyes often went to the children, mafadwi and human.

"Do you want to go home now, Zedos?" she asked, trying to speak loudly enough to get his attention without seeming to shout.

He shook his head. "Bad men. Mommy safe here."

"Oh?" This from Lutanawa, though Ir was obviously interested as well. Nothing had been said of why they had shown up here and nothing had been asked.

"We were set upon in the streets," she said. Would Ir know what a street was? She amended it to, "On a trail. Zedos whisked us away to safety. I left a man behind. I would at least wish to know if he lives."

"Augun?" asked Zedos and disappeared at once. He reappeared in seconds with a bandaged and bewildered man lying beside him. Whisked from bed, most likely. "Augun good!" he proclaimed.

"Now what did we tell you about bringing people without asking?" said Ramapee. Qala did not mind. She was only happy the former pirate survived.

Zedos laughed. "Put back." And he did. But he was steadfast about not returning his mother to danger.

"I do not envy your next few years," spoke Lutanawa. Ir snickered. Mothers everywhere know about difficult children.

"You stay? So can do," the mafadwi offered.

"Better they come to my house," Lutanawa said. "Would you like that, Zedos?"

"Alright." He sounded tired.

"Through a gate?" asked Qala. That was the typical shortcut in this world.

"I am barred. Budo thinks I will use them to misbehave." She offered no further explanation. Goodbyes were made and out into the dusk they followed the goddess. Dusk was as beautiful as noon, and noon was as beautiful as dawn and night. It made Qala's heart ache to breath the air of this world, to watch its moons rise, to simply know it existed.

"My palanquin," announced the goddess. Two quite huge mafadwi squatted by the conveyance, which was surprisingly simple and constructed of bamboo. They climbed in and the bearers began to carry them away. Faster, faster, the jungle beside their way becoming a blur. Out of the valley, onward into lower lying land, thick with scented jungle. The white and yellow flowers were shooting stars as they passed. The true stars were beginning to appear in the sky when they jolted to a halt.

That smell. The sea? "This is my home," said Lutanawa.

It was not unlike the house of Mawa, the only other building Qala had ever seen in the world of Krat. Post and beam, thatched roof, mat walls. The sort of structure that was common in the southern isles of her own word. Its veranda faced a wide golden beach. The sea beyond was dark. Qala felt a great desire to see it at sunrise.

Ramapee moved close. "Was it right to trust this woman?"

"I do not think she means us harm. I do think she may not get along that well with the other gods."

The pair followed Lutanawa up the broad stairs. "Do you two share a sleeping mat?" she asked, offhandedly, at the top.

Qala was quick to let her know they did not. The goddess tipped her head at Ramapee. "There is room on mine if you wish." She said no more but walked on.

Was that why she had brought them here? Something as simple and as human as a seduction? "You needn't accept," she whispered to the priestess.

"I — I would rather share yours, Qala."

There it was. She had known, of course, but ignored it all. She put her arm about the woman and that became an embrace. "Not here, I think. Not now." If only because it might arouse jealousy in this goddess.

Something scampered by them. A tiny mafadwi? Not a child, she was fairly certain. "My servants," Lutanawa informed them. "The rest of the family does not approve of me breeding mafadwi for my own purposes." It returned. Rather, he returned. The mafadwi stood about waist height. Small horns curled back from a receding forehead. It bleated something. "They don't speak, of course. But it did let me know a meal is being prepared."

They followed her into a spacious, high-ceilinged room, the light of the oil lamps barely allowing them to make out the massive roof beams. "We can have beer while we wait. Sit here, on either side of me." Lutanawa took a place at the end of a long woven mat.

The beer appeared in wooden bowls. It was uncommonly good. "I believe, Looty," remarked Qala, "that is the best thing I have ever consumed in this world." The meals in her relatives' abodes had tended to blandness.

"I am not sated with existence as are some," the goddess replied. "I enjoy all the flavors of life." She sat quietly for a moment. "That may change, I know. I may become as the others, lost in their pointless immortality."

Two of the little mafadwi servants brought bowls of fruit. "Xido has found a way to avoid it," Qala said.

"By living among mortals? I fear that may hurt too much but maybe I'll try it. In time. Now tell me of what led you to this point. Attacked, you say? Why?"

There was no reason not to lay out the whole story, and it would fill the time. More courses appeared, fish and flesh and starchy vegetables of some sort. It proved necessary to stop frequently and explain this or that. Lutanawa knew amazingly little of mortal life.

She had only one more question at the end.

"This Galana. She is your lover?"

How had she jumped to that? But it might be best to admit to the fact. "She was. No more, but I feel an obligation."

"I understand that." The goddess continued to stuff herself long after her guests were filled and over-filled. Zedos had fallen asleep beside his mother.

Lutanawa leaned back, finished at last. Maybe like a snake she only ate now and again, Qala thought, and it had to last a while.

"I have decided," the goddess proclaimed, "to help you rescue this captive."

41.

Mawa was watching the sun rise over the waters. "This place is too open for me," she said. "But it can be pleasant."

Qala took a seat beside her, Zedos in her lap. "I wondered which of you would be the first to show up. Looty does know you're here?"

"There is no way I could prevent her knowing. I'm sure she'll come out and greet me in a while." For the first time, the goddess turned her eyes from the sea. "She has offered you no harm, has she?"

"Only made a pass at Ramapee. That might have harmed my heart a little." It sounded foolish as soon as she said it.

"Ah. I am glad of this, my friend, and wish you both well. But if my niece has become enamored of her, she could be dangerous."

"You are all dangerous," Qala had to point out.

"Indeed. Looty gets along better with me than the others. That is why I am the one here now."

"Not her father?"

"Him least of all." Mawa stared into the distance for some time before going on. "You two are kindred spirits. Headstrong and nihilistic and ever seeking."

"But I have found purpose at last, in my son."

"Perhaps in another, as well? Lutanawa had purpose in a child for a while. I think his loss hurt her badly, led her to blame all existence."

An existence she could not escape herself, being immortal. Could gods commit suicide? Qala had no idea.

"Ah, there you are. Breakfast is being prepared." Lutanawa took a place beyond Mawa. "So what do you intend for my guests, Spider?"

"I intend to take them home. To their own world."

"Someone may prevent you," replied Lutanawa. Her smirk spoke of secret knowledge.

"You know you can not match any one of us."

"Not me, my eight-legged aunt. Zedos. He will not go and I think none of us can force him." She sounded decidedly amused now. "He has decided his mom is safer here."

Mawa digested this. "She and Ramapee will bounce back on their own in time."

"And Zedos is likely to just send them here again. So —" Her tone became conspiratorial. "I intend to interest him in an adventure. We will go and teach those bad men a lesson and he can see how his mom can whip them. With a little help."

"A spider and a snake?" asked Mawa.

"I suppose you can tag along."

"Oh, there you all are." Ramapee looked with some curiosity toward Mawa, not expecting her there. She had met her but once, hadn't she? In Flawum's keep.

"We might as well spread our breakfast here on the porch," said Lutanawa. She clapped her hands; a small mafadwi — not so diminutive nor as hairy as those who served the night before — came. It was also capable of some speech, answering its mistress in monosyllables. In a minute, a mat was unrolled. Bowls of food followed.

Qala noted their host touched little of it this morning. Lutanawa was thinking of something and it probably had nothing to do with her.

At last, she addressed her aunt. "I saw the little mafadwi girl Jong yesterday. Not a mafadwi, maybe."

"As we also have come to wonder." Mawa was not going to reveal much, not right away.

"She is immortal. You know I have a gift for seeing that. And I am told she can travel between worlds on her own."

"Two of the three things we might say are necessary to be a god. But will she achieve the third?" Mawa chose a ripe golden fruit from one of the baskets.

"The third may not be necessary. But I think she will learn to divide her natures."

"It is long since a god was born of mafadwi. Not since the times of chaos, perhaps." Her gaze became distant. She would remember those days, the days before Lutanawa was born. "Did you see the other children? What thought you?"

"Their human heritage predominates over that of the Ancient Ones. I do not think they will ever be more than mafadwi."

Mawa nodded. "I agree," she said and took a bite of her fruit. "Damn, Looty, why doesn't anything this tasty grow near my house?"

"Not enough sunlight." Qala thought that entirely likely.

"Your family seems rather unruly compared to the Ildin gods, if you don't mind me saying so," spoke Ramapee.

"Your deities are extraordinarily well-behaved," admitted Mawa. "Even the evil ones."

Lutanawa nodded. "We do not deny our failings. But there are worse out there."

"Far worse. In infinite worlds, how could there not be?"

"All in all," spoke Qala, "you seem no worse than the gods of the Sharshites."

"That is because we interact less with mortals," Lutanawa said. "You just don't know us as well."

"And your own Muram gods are not such a wonderful bunch," Mawa pointed out.

"Well do I know it! Maybe I should switch to Kamat when I return home."

"A most excellent choice," felt Ramapee.

"And what of the shrine you promised me?" asked a bell-like voice.

"Esefa? How got you past my wards?" Lutanawa was perhaps more perturbed than surprised.

"Trade secret, my girl." She looked at Zedos and winked.

"I bringed her!" he crowed.

"My little man on the inside, opening the door. I wanted to check on you two. It seems I may have finally gotten it right this time."

Both Mawa and Lutanawa let their eyes go from Esefa to Qala to Ramapee and back again. "If you are involved, I will most certainly step far aside," announced Lutanawa.

"She is your type. I recognize this," spoke the queen of the Sharshite gods. "But it seems that is also Qala's type. And you — I think maybe you truly prefer men."

"There's time enough for both," maintained Lutanawa. "That's how it is with gods. You know that."

"Even we shall run out of time," stated Esefa, and disappeared into shifting shards of light.

Lutanawa shrugged. "So it is. We shall still go and rescue your Lady

Galana, and thrash those bad men who attacked you most thoroughly. Won't we, Zedos?

"Yeah! Kill 'em all." He reached out somewhere and retrieved a sword. It was too long, too heavy, for him to hold, and clattered onto the bamboo deck.

"Put that back, young man!" ordered Mawa. "We do not take things unless we must."

Lutanawa gave her a somewhat cynical look but spoke not. "Important things, anyway," the Spider added. "Someone's life might depend on that sword."

"Or an innocent might be killed with it."

"We'll get you a sword of your own when we go home," Qala promised, "and I will teach you how to use it." And to sail and to ride and all the rest she had been planning.

Maybe this somewhat demure priestess of Kamat would be by her side in all that. Qala could only hope and go on.

42.

"We shall go and rescue the beautiful lady — she is beautiful Zedos, isn't she? — and smite all your mother's enemies. Maybe I'll eat the Pirate King!"

"I would strongly caution you against changing form in another world," said Mawa. "Like your Uncle Xido you might wander around that way for years. Centuries, even."

"More likely, I'd lie up and digest him for a couple months."

Mawa had no answer for that. "The great problem," she announced, "is knowing the exact spot to travel to in your world." Mawa may have seemed to say this to both of them but she was truly addressing Qala. She was the one who knew the place.

She sighed. "I don't even have a map." And didn't trust those that existed in her world. "How do we find it?"

"You gave us a pretty good approximation. Looty and I shall have to scout from there. We can take turns narrowing it down, sending part of ourselves to different spots along the coast."

"It's too bad neither of us can stand on the water and get a wider view! Not in this form, anyway," said Lutanawa. "Once we discover that cove and that village, we can go right on in and find the room where she is held captive. Even unlock the door."

"Easier to do that sort of thing when we're on the scene."

"It would seem simpler to set me down on a trim little sailboat and let me approach that way."

"But much more risky," Mawa felt, "and time-consuming. We know we won't be seen this way. Ah, if only Xido were with us! He knows this sort of thing but we can't trust him with our plans."

"He'd try to stop them for sure," said Lutanawa.

"Oh, Xido knows where you are, Qala. We talked this morning and I told him you were safe. Whether I believe that or not."

"So we have one more problem," Lutawana said, lowering her voice to a whisper. "Zedos. He's gone to sleep hasn't he?"

"So it seems," said the boy's mother.

"He will insist on coming and I'm not sure we can stop him."

"I will not take Zedos along. His life is more important to me than

Galana's." Or a treaty or any of the rest. Were Qala offered transport home for her son and herself at this moment, back to Melawhem, she might just accept it.

"It shouldn't take more than a hour or two. Maybe only minutes," Mawa said. "We could be in and out during the night, while the boy slept."

"One of you would have to remain and watch over him," Qala stated. "There can be no argument to this." Ramapee was trustworthy but this was not her world.

Lutanawa nodded. "This is so. Which of us will it be?"

It took no real time for her to decide. "This was Looty's idea, so she should come with me. And I do trust you more, Mawa, to keep an eye on the boy. No offense, Looty, but I know too little of you."

"As long as I'm going on the adventure you can insult me all day!"

Such a romantic for a goddess. One might think her a young girl but she had centuries, millennia of life behind her. Maybe it took longer for deities to mature. Or going by Lenco, maybe they never did.

And now she was looking forward to the daring rescue of a fair maiden. Qala hoped Lutanawa knew how to use weapons.

It was not until the next afternoon that Mawa came out of a trance to announce she found their target. "It helped that your Quso was there. Zedos did a pretty good job of showing me what he looked like."

"Your were in the boy's mind?" Lutanawa did not seem to like that at all. "You shouldn't go poking around. And he's just a little boy."

"A little boy who fell into the wizard link without problem. That is yet another thing he must be taught."

"Absolutely. The ability could be a great danger to him." She fell silent, pensive.

"What is it, Looty?" asked her aunt.

The goddess sniffed but once. "I only remembered other links, in other times. Mortals who are gone."

"Your son," murmured Mawa.

"His father too."

"Oh! Im still lives. Xido was speaking with him only a few days ago. But," she admitted, "he is very aged."

164

"I do not think I would want to see him so. Better to remember him young and powerful, as he was when Xido brought him here."

All this seemed quite astonishing and quite interesting and quite useless to Qala. Get these wagons back on the road! "So we can go. Immediately."

"Why not? Tonight should do — hmm, I should have checked the moon and the tides, shouldn't I? And whether night will be same time there as here."

"Late in the third quarter for the moon," said Qala, "but rising fairly early this time of year. I was just there, after all. And the tides — yes, they should be high enough." If they got going early enough. The tides didn't matter all that much anyway, as they were not going by boat. "As for day and night, I have no idea."

"We'll look," promised Lutanawa. "Mawa has to show me the way."

"After supper? I'm tired."

"Now," insisted her niece. "Let's get it done and move on."

"Will it be harder to find in the dark?" asked Qala as the two goddesses prepared.

"Not if we already know where it is," answered Mawa, and both went into their trance, sitting quietly, breathing steadily. One would not guess they had sent a part of themselves into another world.

"Good," said Mawa, opening her eyes. "The time is pretty well synchronized at the moment."

"The two worlds tend to drift apart in time and then catch back up. We don't notice it, of course," added Lutanawa, "when we are here."

"But there is a bond of some sort between the two." Mawa laughed. "Lenco might say we are the bond, the gods of two worlds, and if we did not visit there they would drift apart completely."

Lutanawa scowled at the mention of her father's name. "Let's eat," she said, "and then do this. You know, one of us could go tend to it without you, Qala. Or we could show Xido the proper location and leave it to him."

"Do you think that would be best?" She might be a little disappointed not being the one to rescue Galana, but only a little.

"I'd rather have you there, given the choice," the goddess responded. "It feels right."

"And Qala may have knowledge you need," added Mawa. That sounded reasonable to all three. "Remember," the goddess continued, "Galana will have to be returned to her world through a gate, once we get her here. Otherwise, the lady would be pulled back, in time, to her place of captivity." Qala did remember how that worked. They could worry about it after the rescue mission.

All seemed to go well. A good meal, a sleepy Zedos settled down with Mawa to keep a close watch on him. Qala buckled on her sword and both of her knives. "I'm ready, Looty," she whispered. The goddess placed a hand on her shoulder and then they were rushing forward to somewhere. She remembered to close her eyes, as Budo and Lenco had suggested when they first transported her from one world to another.

A dark street. No moon to speak of? Ah, the skies were clouded. The houses along the dirt way were naught but hovels, some built of drift-wood. But up there, on the slope above them, a blocky stone building. Not tall enough to call a tower, maybe. That was where they held Galana.

The single drowsy guard before the rough door succumbed to a swift knife in his side, quickly followed by another across the throat. There was no noise. Looty was looking at her somewhat oddly. Maybe she hadn't expected this sort of thing. But this sort of thing was necessary.

A dim light from a room somewhere in the back, a candle most likely. Galana was up the stairs, Mawa had assured them, though she had not taken her niece that far on their reconnaissance. The steps squeaked beneath their feet, but this entire edifice seemed to squeak and moan and grumble, the sounds coming from a hundred directions at once. Was that someone singing down there? Maybe sitting in the kitchen by that candlelight they glimpsed.

To the left. The door was locked. As expected. "Your task, Looty," she whispered. Qala knew the goddess had been practicing this skill, a skill she needed not at all in her normal life. Xido had explained it to her once — he sent a part of himself around through another world to unlock the door from the other side. It was not easy.

"What?" whispered Lutanawa. "There is a spell on the lock. Humph, not a very good one. There!" The door swung open. They could see someone sit up in the bed, against the dim light of a barred window.

"It's me, Galana," whispered Qala. "We'll get you out of here." She carefully shut the door behind her before finding a candle.

"Allow me," said the goddess, pulling a flame to herself and lighting the taper. They could clearly see the noblewoman sitting up and not that much worse for wear. "Who is that?" demanded Lutanawa.

"Why, it is the Lady Galana," Qala was not sure what the problem was.

"But she is — old!" The goddess's displeasure and disappointment was evident. "And ugly. Fah!" And she disappeared.

Qala stared at the empty spot for only a second before turning back. "I would say we are on our own," she told Galana.

43.

The only course was to steal a boat and sail away from here. That might not be so difficult. No large ships moored at the little cove below this village. They would sit offshore to be loaded and stay no longer than necessary.

"What was the problem with your friend?" asked Galana as they crept toward the water.

"I can only assume she expected a fresh young maiden. We never thought to tell her otherwise." Maybe she even hoped to seduce her.

How soon would Mawa know how things went? Looty might not even have gone back to her house. Zedos would know something was wrong by morning and look for her. Probably find her too. She would rather that not happen.

"I remember a break in the cliffs here somewhere," said Qala. "It's been a while since I saw this place."

"They brought me up to the village through a cleft. There were guards stationed at it."

Undoubtedly, there would be still. The cliffs were not all that high, really, maybe thrice her height. Too far to jump and too far for Galana to try to climb down. She wished now the moon were not hidden, so they might find the way and assess the dangers.

"It was, um, to the right side. Of the beach, that is."

"So we go left," Qala said. "There should be a well-worn path." How close was the cliff? It would be too easy to blunder over it in the dark! The only way to know their direction was the faint outline of the hills rising behind the village.

A muffled exclamation for Galana. Where was she?

"Fell flat on my face," said the woman. "Watch out, there's a drop there." Qala felt before her with one foot. A step or two more and she would have gone over too. "I think this is your pathway," Galana continued.

Qala slipped down the bank. Less than a couple feet, not a cliff but dangerous enough in the dark! Yes, this was the trail. She could feel the ruts made by wagon wheels, transporting whatever goods passed through here to and from the way down to the cove.

Forward, cautiously. A sentry was more likely at the bottom of the passage than the top, but she could not depend on that. Ah, there was a bit of moon showing through the clouds, and the bright stars.

And there seemed a very faint, a barely-to-be-seen light coming from below. It must be rising from the beach end of the cleft, a shuttered lantern perhaps. "We're there," whispered Qala. "Now to get down." The passage proved easy of transit. Someone had dumped and smoothed enough rubble and sand to make a gently descending ramp. One might even be able to get a wheelbarrow or small cart through it. But it would need frequent maintenance and, as Qala remembered, items more often were hoisted and lowered over the cliffs. This way was mostly for human traffic.

No sentry at the top. She had been right, there. No one expected trouble from that direction. Qala would have posted a guard despite that. Their way became clearer, both from the celestial light above and the small lamp below. A man sat beside it, whittling at a piece of driftwood.

Thoroughly engrossed in it, too. They might be able to slip by — she would as soon not need kill the fellow. That could make too much noise. "Keep to the left wall," she whispered. There was less concealing shadow there but the sentry was on the right, so it was the only choice. His post would offer more shade during the day, ever a consideration for those who must sit outside.

The mouth of the crevice was relatively broad. They were a good thirty feet distant from the guard as they slipped past and onto the darkened sand. "Remain cautious and quiet," Qala warned her companion. "There are sure to be men on the beach."

But sleeping men, it was to be hoped. Visitors would prefer not to stay in the village above. The villagers undoubtedly felt the same about it. She could make out the dark forms of boats pulled up onto the beach. As anticipated, the tide was fairly high. That would make launching one easier. "We need one with a sail," she said, perhaps more to herself than Galana. "Some of these are boats rowed in from larger vessels." She looked out across black waters, lying languid this night. "We can be sure those vessels are out there."

Not too large. There would be only the two of them to push it off the shore. This one, maybe. The water lapped at its stern and, yes, a mast and sail were stowed in it. It hardly seemed a practical craft for any who lived here.

Ouch. She felt about the bottom, gingerly. Fishing lines and hooks. The boat made more sense now. Maybe its owner simply liked to sail for the sake of sailing, too. Qala could almost feel guilty for stealing it. Silently, the women pushed it out, set it afloat, clambered in. "Paddle for now. Slowly and as quietly as you can." Once they got out a way, more vigorous rowing would be called for, and she could raise the sail. Qala hoped she would not be pulled back to Krat's world while they were still at sea. That was a chance they would have to take. Best not to mention it to Galana.

What loomed up before them, darkness on darkness? Boats. One, two of them that Qala could see. A challenge. Three boats now, each filled with men, around them, blocking them. Someone held a lantern high.

A voice rang out over the water. "Ah, Qala, an unexpected pleasure!" Quso himself. "Now turn your vessel back to the shore, if you please."

There was no choice but to obey. They were surrounded by the pirates as soon as they set foot on the sand. "Someone get her weapons," barked Quso.

None seemed eager to make the attempt. "She's one of us," came from the dark. "Qala's entitled to carry her blade."

Quso glared in the direction of the voice. "And I'm entitled to put an arrow through her, aye, and the Sharshite too."

"I'll hand them over," Qala replied.

"Both knives," demanded the pirate leader. "I know you're fond of hiding the one away."

They marched their captives up the beach, to just below the cliffs. "I'll not complain to your jailers until the morrow, Lady Galana," spoke Quso. "No point in rousing the town. Someone get a fire going!"

A driftwood bonfire was soon ablaze. It was not large but still seemed foolhardy to Qala. Attention should not be attracted to this place. She and Galana had not been bound — none had been willing, though Quso might have preferred them so — but were sat down right up against the rocky face of the bluff. No direction to run from there and too many watchful eyes if they did attempt it.

A pair of pirates slowly moved to a spot near them, their eyes on the fire and their comrades. One spoke. "There's some none too happy with Quso as king. There's some what might back a challenge from you, Qala."

"Profits is not so good," added the other.

To rule again? It was not something Qala desired but it might prove the best way out of this mess. "Quso would not face me in combat. His followers would cut me down first."

"Not if you have yer own followers."

"My own weapons would be handy too."

"Aye, that can be managed. Think on it." The two strolled casually away.

Through the next hour, she observed small clumps of men, two or three at a time, gathering and coming apart. Whispered exchanges. They were sounding out who might support a coup, who would risk backing Qala over Quso. It would be dangerous if they failed. Also dangerous if any whiff of it reached the Pirate King.

There were more than thirty pirates on the beach. Hardly a good start for a rebellion and more likely to be Quso loyalists than not. All from his own ship? She guessed it more likely two pirate vessels lay offshore. Quso was too protective of his own skin to sail alone. Too, some of these men had already been ashore before he landed.

The leader stood up and looked her way. He seemed steadier on his feet than most of his men, who had been at an amphora of wine. Quso was never a drinker, she remembered. He liked to stay alert. "Bring the woman!" he called out. "Qala, not the other. She must face pirate judgment."

So he was going to put a legal stamp on his action, here with this many witnesses. He surely intended her death, without delay.

"Qala," he spoke, putting on an orator's manner, turning his head toward his men rather than his captive, "you are charged with betraying your trust. We can forget the fact that you fled your position as queen. That only opened the way for me!" That brought the laughs he intended.

"But now you work against us, seeking to close the ports to our trade. This is treason!"

That did not bring the response for which he hoped. A couple half-hearted cheers were drowned out by a sea of murmurings.

It was as good a time as any to make her own case. "You are wrong to oppose this treaty. Arlak-Port will be more open to you under Flawum than the Mura. Certainly, fewer questions will be asked about merchandise." She was not sure of this but very much expected things to develop that way. And she could advise the new celos to help it along. "It might hurt some smugglers," Qala admitted, in an offhanded manner, "but not our brotherhood."

"Those are our partners and our friends," countered Quso. "Should we betray them?"

"No friends of mine," came a voice. The murmurs suggested general agreement.

"And are we to become the lapdogs of this Sharshite, this would-be king?" snarled Quso. This hit a lot closer to the pirates' true sentiments. They did love their freedom. What they saw as freedom. Qala had loved it herself, until her position as queen turned into its own form of slavery.

Seeing he would never get them more on his side than at the moment, Quso cried out, "I shall pronounce sentence —"

"Not if another rules here!" called another voice. "I'm for Qala, Queen of Pirates!"

For the most part, that was followed by silence.

44.

Someone handed Qala her sword. She saw the mob of pirates divide, some moving toward her, some toward Quso. More than a few seemed unable or unwilling to decide.

"So you got yourself into trouble. I should apologize, shouldn't I?" Lutanawa stood by her side.

"Helping us now would be worth more than any apology. Can you get us out of here?"

"And miss this fight? It looks like great fun! Which one is this Pirate King?"

Qala pointed him out. What was this fickle deity going to do?

"Ah. Not much to look at, is he? I went and sat on a mountaintop for a couple hours and realized what an idiot I am. So I came back."

"We thank you for that, my lady," said Galana.

"And you are better to look at than I realized. Oh well. I think they are waiting for you to make a move, Qala."

Her side was outnumbered, with maybe a dozen men arrayed behind her. Maybe Looty would even up the odds. Qala raised her sword to signal the attack. There was no other course of action available.

Suddenly, Lutanawa was no longer at her side — not as the lithe goddess she knew. A massive snake raised its head, spread its hood, to peer toward Quso. The Pirate King gasped, immediately turned and fled toward the boats, the giant golden cobra following.

She really is going to eat him, thought Qala. Most swords had been lowered. The two factions no longer glowered at each other. What was the point? "Qala!" called out someone. Other voices repeated it, took up the name. This was not what she wanted either. Preferable to being executed, to be sure, but she would rather go home.

A small form appeared before them, stepping out of the shadowed night, a grinning Zedos. "Mommy!" he called. "Galana!" He giggled. "Galana-banana! Go."

He held out his hands and each woman took one. A moment later they were standing before Lutanawa's house, shining silver in the light of the twin moons. Mawa rushed out to them.

"I was watching for you from the porch. And I thought you were in bed!" she told Zedos.

"Had to save Mommy. And Galana-banana." He laughed longer this time.

"That's not a nice name for your mommy's friend," admonished the goddess.

"It's alright with me," said the noblewoman. "He can call me that anytime. If Sesa doesn't give me a grandson soon, I may just steal this boy."

"Looty?"

"She remains behind. In snake form."

Mawa only sighed at this news. "I knew something was wrong when it took so long. Then she refused to answer when I called to her."

"Looty hided," spoke Zedos. He gave his mother a rather accusatory look. "Mommy too."

"It's a good thing you found me," Qala said. "Let's not play hide-and-seek again for a while. And lets get inside where we can tell our tales."

"What's all the noise?" Ramapee had come out onto the veranda. "Oh, you're all back. And you got the little one out of bed?"

Qala had to laugh at her disapproving tone. "He got himself out and traveled to another world while you slept." She turned to her son, knelt down to speak face-to-face. "You know it's safe for Mommy to go home now."

"After breagfuss. Little mafadwi fix." He turned toward the house and chirped something Qala could not understand. From her look, neither could Mawa. "Ready soon," he said, seemingly quite satisfied.

"How did you learn to speak to them?" asked Mawa, as they entered.

"Looty teached me. When Looty gum back, Mommy?"

"I'm not sure, my dear. She has, um, business to attend to." To digest, more likely.

"It may do her some good to be the cobra for a time," felt Mawa. "Though we might hope she doesn't swallow too many mortals in the meantime."

"If they are as bad as that Quso, she is welcome to them," declared

Lady Galana. "Oh, what have we here? Monkeys?" The tiny mafadwi servants had appeared with bowls and baskets of food. Lots of fruit. Maybe Zedos had asked for it.

"Mongey-mafadwi," the boy laughed. "Little mongey-mafadwi."

Qala noted Mawa slowly nodding. Maybe there was something to the observation. The various stories — or different versions of the same story, more properly — were told over the next hour.

"I think," concluded Qala, "Looty made up for her desertion the best way she knew how. I hope she does not remain a snake overlong. And I hope she decides to visit her old lover while she is in his world."

"He might be the one who could bring her back from beast-shape," spoke Mawa. "If he used those jewels they used to call Xido. Otherwise, her mind can not be reached, not by any of us."

She looked at her nephew, gnawing at an oblong ruby-skinned fruit and then at the Lady Galana. "You do not seem to be linked to your world at all. This must somehow be the doing of Zedos but I do not understand it."

"So Galana will not need pass through a gate?" asked Qala.

"No. She should be able to go directly home." Mawa again regarded the little boy. "If Zedos takes her. Are you ready to take them back, Zedos?"

"Home?" he asked.

"No, the place where we slept last." It seemed likely their friends would still be there.

"I shall tell Xido you are on the way. If he'll answer." Mawa was else-where only a moment. "He knows. I'll stay a little while, just in case Looty comes back."

"Bye little mongey-mafadwi," called Zedos. "Bye Aunt Mawa." He stood between Ramapee and his mother, offering each a small hand. A few vertiginous seconds later they stood in a dark room. "Damana?" asked Zedos of the darkness. "I taged you to Damana, Mommy."

It must be one of the tack rooms at the hostelry. Yes, she could make out dim shapes, saddles, shovels, buckets. And in the corner, two figures who had pulled up a blanket to shield themselves. "Hi, deary," called Damana. "You brought your mom back?"

175

"Yep! No more bad men now!" He was proud of his part, to be sure. Qala did doubt the part about no more bad men.

"Where's the door?" she asked. "I do believe we are intruding, Lady Galana. Horos, you can report to me later. I can see you are far too busy at the moment."

"Yes, ma'am," he choked out as she stepped into the morning sunlight.

45.

"Augun. I wish to know of Augun," was Qala's first request. She had left him lying in a muddy street of Arlak-Port. Yes, Zedos had brought him to her, seemingly on the repair, but she wanted more.

"Back on his feet," reported Ranwif. "He claims to have had a strange dream about seeing you in another world."

Maybe it was best he went on thinking it a dream. "Pain does strange things to the mind," she allowed.

Ranwif obviously did not believe that at all. He made no comment.

"Where is Xit?" she asked. "He should have received a message to expect us."

"With Nedos on his ship. So is Augun, for that matter. Um, messages — we should send one to Lord Vullum, shouldn't we?"

"To Flawum. Send it to Flawum. He can inform Galana's husband. We can trust Corad to send messages on to Domi and Sarowhem." Yes, that was all that was needed. "We may turn home, now, Ranwif. In a day or two."

"None too soon," felt the young equester. "Here comes our missing boy. Alone. I don't know why he and Damana pretend they are not together."

"They were very together the last I saw of them. I'm thinking he might take your position some day, my lad."

Ranwif grinned. "And Damana my wife's?"

Damana as bailiff? That she was not nearly so sure of. "I am hoping to have another to help me," she said. Ranwif seemed to have no idea whom she meant. He would learn soon enough. Or it would all evaporate and not matter.

"And is the Cana still with us? I know she wished to travel on and visit more of her people." Those she called her people, people of another nation. But Qala named Sharshites her people these days.

"She waited for you. And for her aide, of course."

"Of course. Then Ramapee is with her now?" The woman had disappeared almost at once. That weighed on Qala's heart.

"She is. Hi, Horos. Ready to take the afternoon guard?"

"Yes, sir."

"But sit down and eat first," spoke Qala, "and let Old Lady Qala speak wisdom to you. Marry that girl as soon as you can. Don't wait, don't hesitate."

"She's just waiting for you to ask," added Ranwif.

The young man blushed, but only a little. "You think so? She'd want me?"

"That she has already proven. Now you must prove you want her," Qala told him. "What is keeping Lady Galana? Maybe she really does intend to kidnap my son!"

They were arrayed along one of the trestle tables set up in the court-yard for use by any and all lodgers. An open stand across the way offered food through most of the day, at reasonable enough prices. Greasy though, and not to compare with Benaro's. Ha, if Damana were made bailiff she would reign over her big brother. Best avoid that maybe!

"They come, my lady," spoke Ranwif, nodding in their direction. "And Damana with them." Qala noted that one of the Sharshite guardsmen followed at a discreet distance. Probably Ranwif's doing, though Horos might have ordered the same had he not been preoccupied. "And Xit too, I believe." He gazed toward the far end of the compound.

Qala turned. "Nedos and Augun as well. Who is that with them?"

"One of the captain's men, most likely. He has felt the need of a guard since your incident."

"We need more room. Bring one of the other trestles over. And Damana, go buy some more food." She handed the girl sufficient coinage to cover a large meal. "You know you could help her carry it, Horos."

"Yes, come along, you," she ordered.

Ranwif watched the two walk away. "They may be engaged by the time they get back with the food. Give Horos an idea and he'll act on it."

"It took forever with you and Domi. And here are the last of our party." Lura and Ramapee approached from the other direction. They might have been at the stables. Preparing to go.

It was necessary to repeat all their tale. Galana went first. "Those brutes that grabbed me hurried me south, changing horses more than once. They were organized. And a wizard joined them. I can recognize them. Or I can recognize when they go off to talk with someone far away."

Qala broke in. "Looty, er, Lutanawa said there was a spell on your lock. A sorcerer must have been there in that village."

"Hmm, not the one I saw. He turned back north after a while. They blindfolded me later but I could tell we were on a boat. On the Arlak seems likely. And then onto a ship and another boat and a dark locked room till I was rescued. Twice!"

"Twice?" asked Xido.

"Once by Qala and her friend, and then by your son. He did rather the better job of it."

"I am afraid Looty didn't prove very trustworthy," murmured Qala.

"I could have told you that. While you were about your own adventures, I decided to follow you down to visit Nedos. Instead I found a bloody Augun staggering out of an alley."

"Good thing he did," said the Mur. "These Arlak folk would just as soon have robbed me and throwed me back in."

"So I carried him down to the ship." Not a difficult task for Xido, despite Augun's bulk. This Qala knew. "Nedos and I patched him up. He recovered. That's pretty much it." He winked. "Except for one strange hallucination. We could really make no more plans right then and you came back pretty quickly, when it comes down to it. And successfully too."

"This sorcerer that was mentioned," broke in the Cana. "Or two sorcerers, perhaps? They serve the Pirate King, I assume."

"Served," said Qala. "I am pretty sure it is served now."

"Ah. I will not celebrate any man's death but we know there was an alliance between Quso and the Wizard-Lord. His death will at least disrupt that."

Damana and Horos returned, burdened with food and drink. To her credit, the girl carried her fair share. As they passed it out, Qala began her own tale. Not all the details to be sure. Zedos busied himself with lunch, seeming to pay little attention.

179

At the end of the story, his father gave him a long look, a hard look. "He does indeed need to be trained. I am not certain I am the one to take charge."

"You have trained many a wizard," came Lura's soft voice. "Including Im."

"But most were adults. And none had godlike powers."

"He is not a god."

"A demigod. Mortal. He might not even be a particularly skillful sorcerer. I am not so good myself when I become fully mortal."

Qala nodded. "I remember. So should we enlist your brother?"

"I am sure you mean Budo. I would not entrust anyone to Lenco." No one disagreed. "Yes, maybe Budo. He needs to teach the little mafadwi girl too."

"Then there is no need for any of us to linger in this town," spoke Lura. "I and my guards will travel east tomorrow, to further spread my message." She smiled at the woman by her side. "My Ramapee has decided to join her fate to another."

"Please keep the horses I have lent you," Qala said. "Return them if and when you can."

"Ah, I am getting four steeds in trade for you, you my girl." The Ildin woman could not prevent a rather foolish smile from appearing.

"Perhaps five," spoke Xido. "If you permit me, Mec Lura, I shall accompany you and your people across the mountains."

46.

"Are you sure you are able to ride?" she asked. Augun's condition was the only thing that might prevent them leaving on the morrow. Lura and Xido had departed this morning. Nedos would sail shortly.

"As able as ever, ma'am, considering I'm a seaman."

Qala knew well what he meant. She would never feel as comfortable on the back of an animal as she did on the deck of a ship. "If you start bleeding, we will leave you behind," she let him know.

"As you should. Um, I've been thinking some, my lady," he started, hesitated, started again. "There's only one fellow I've ever, well, maybe said things to. Things I shouldn't have let slip." Qala waited. The man would say what he intended, eventually. "That would be Lovi."

The head cook at Sarowhem, and his lover. And himself a Mur who might have had ties to piracy. Qala had not been sure about that, only that Lovi had been a seaman. A cook on a vessel, anyway.

"Not wise, but I do know things happen," she replied. "It is something to look into when we return home." Or mention to Corad when they reached Flawum's keep.

She missed having Lura there, and Xido too. They could have reached out to Looty maybe, or to Im and Saj, and done something for her. Not one in the party traveling north had wizardly skills, much less godlike ones.

Well, except Zedos, of course. Who would take charge of him then? She heard nothing from Budo nor any other of Xido's siblings.

The street seemed abuzz with something. Qala had stuck to the main easterly thoroughfare this time. No more alleys in Arlak-Port! Ranwif and one of Flawum's guardsmen followed. It was time to bid Captain Nedos a farewell. For now. She did intend to have a business relationship with the man.

She also intended to tell him her story, so he could pass it on to his wife. Maybe Kataree and Saj and this old wizard Im they all seemed to revere could look into the Lutanawa situation. In fact, she had scrawled a letter to Marana, with many crossings out and smudges, telling of these things. Nedos could surely get that to her.

If anyone could get Saj to act, it would be his wife. They were at the north-south road, the one they would ride tomorrow. South to the docks and Nedos. There seemed to be the same subtle stirring here, a feeling of things happening or about to. Knots of men gathered and there was both shaking and nodding of heads.

"You can feel the tension too, can't you?" she asked Augun.

"Something's up, for sure. Maybe a report of a storm out at sea? It's the season."

It was possible. As soon as Nedos greeted them at his gangplank they learned otherwise. "Have you heard?" he asked. "Someone killed the Pirate King!"

Qala tried to keep from snickering. "I was there when it happened. Quso may even be digested by now. Any word on who might take his place?"

"There were rumors you had reclaimed it." Nedos sounded as if he were almost willing to believe it. "That would be the worst thing to happen to honest sea-merchants I could imagine. You were their greatest leader and the longest to reign."

It was a little flattering. True also. "No interest," she said, following him to a canopy in the stern. There stood a portable desk and some folding canvas chairs. A crock of wine and cups too.

"War is likely if one strong leader doesn't emerge at once." He waved toward the chairs; all but the guardsman took seats. That man preferred to guard, at a little distance.

The man who had approached her on the beach might be one of the contenders. He seemed both ambitious and persuasive. Beyond that, she could not even guess. Nor did she care, except in the sense of wishing to know her enemies. There was no question that pirates were the enemy now. She had and they wanted to take.

"Digested, you say?" Nedos had managed to keep his curiosity under control for only a few minutes. It was time to give him her story.

"I shall certainly tell all to Kataree," he promised at the conclusion. "I do think she will want to let Im know about it. Now," said Nedos, refilling their cups, "how about talking business?"

Not that much could be discussed beyond nebulous plans for future trade through Flawum's yet-to-be kingdom. Wine helped fuel those plans. However, Qala had a feeling her chief investments these coming years, the next two decades, should center on her own estate, preparing it for what might come. Yes, a property here and there might increase her capital but she must always remember such were a means to an end. Melawhem counted. Arlacas did not.

But maybe Arlacana did, the kingdom that would lie to her south. A strong Arlacana would be a wall against trouble from that direction. She did not even know if the empire would survive what was to come. Oh, in some form, Saj thought it would. Its power might no longer reach to her own little realm on the Chas.

She brooded on such things as they trudged back to their lodging. Why hadn't they ridden? Yes, yes, no need to tire the horses today. The sun was slipping low, its light sifting though the narrow alleys, around the weathered gray houses of Arlak-Port. Arlacas. She might as well get used to it. The sand flies were coming out.

"Qala?"

She came out of her reverie. "What is it, Augun?"

"Did your little boy, um, in truth take me to another world?"

"He did. He wanted to prove to me you were alive."

"I didn't see much of it but it was —" His voice trailed off. "Beautiful. It was beautiful. All glittering like jewels. I felt better after. I think I healed more quick-like." Qala could believe that. Just being in that world for a few seconds might have its effects. "The woman was good looking too. Not your Ramapee, the other one. Is it too forward to say so?"

"She is a goddess. I can not speak for her."

"The one who killed Quso?" Augun was not bothered in the least by deities being involved in ones life.

"The very one."

"And a snake now. That's not fitting." He shooks his heavy head. "But she'll change back, someday, right?"

"Right. Did you notice the other —" Qala was not sure how to put it.

"The other woman? The big brown monster? I take it that's little Mong's mom."

"Astute of you."

"Well, the little fellow was right there. I gets along with little Mong."

183

She hadn't realized he'd seen much of the mafadwi. "Much better'n our Muram divils, ain't they?"

"I've never met any of them." And hoped not to.

"There's enough divils walking about and calling themselves men," stated Augun, and spoke no more.

Qala didn't have to speak to agree.

47.

Eight riders, seven horses. They had lost Nedos but gained Galana, and Xido and the Ildin — all but Ramapee — had ridden away on the other five mounts. One Sharshite guard Ranwif had at once dispatched as a messenger, to ride swiftly before them to Flawum. Qala did feel more vulnerable without those Ildin archers bringing up the rear.

But she was happy. Exceptionally, extraordinarily happy. Ramapee rode at her side by day, slept at her side by night. Only her son made her happier.

It was not like the passion she had shared with Galana and a few others over the years. Nor was it the tenderness of Mawa's embrace, the physical skill of Xido's. It was love. She had known love once before, when young, and lost it. She might tell Ramapee of that someday. No need to now. No need to explain anything.

Nor any reason to worry about attacks. The pirates were in disarray, their leader slain. It was unlikely any smugglers were organized enough to make trouble; those had only allied themselves with Quso, let the man seduce them, when it became convenient. They may see now that profit lay elsewhere.

Not a one of these riders was very important. Oh, Lady Galana, to be sure. That was what got her snatched in the first place. But who would even know she was with them? Those who hoped to scuttle the treaty would look to her husband and the others in Flawum's keep.

The second day was as the first, save that they moved away from River Arlak. It is not to be assumed Qala paid no attention to the scrubby country through which they rode. Without the concern of attack weighing heavy on her, she could see it better, see its potentials and drawbacks. That town they had stayed in — yes, that was something to think about.

On they rode and the ground rose. Flatlands gave way to hills. There were people here; small villages were frequent along the way and much of the land under cultivation. Some of it looked tired, especially in the south. Used up. Maybe these Ildin did need to follow the Cana to a new land. In time, Flawum's keep appeared. It was more visible coming from this way, the terrain sloping down from its walls. On the town side, one barely saw the place until one was upon it.

There must be a good view from this side. She should look for it and protest being stuck into another windowless room. Indeed, she had hardly entered that side of the place at all. Even Flawum's suite was over on the far side. Also on the interior, having no view at all. No way to live!

Lady Galana was whisked away to her husband at once. "I'm surprised an escort wasn't sent south to meet us," whispered Ranwif. "I would have ordered one."

"Me too," agreed Qala. "It's lax. You should mention it to Flawum. But not to Vullum. Are we where we were before?" she asked their escort. She was fairly certain it was the same man.

"We've shuffled things about a little, my lady. The celos felt Lord Vullum and his wife should have a room of their own. It, um, is a little better than yours." He sounded politely apologetic, but not at all embarrassed.

"Does it have windows?" she asked.

Ranwif answered that at once. "All the rooms are windowless on the first two floors. A hallway wraps around the perimeter of each floor, with many windows to let in the light. A room that opens onto one of those hallways is desirable, but they are largely taken up by Flawum's functionaries."

She might have known he would be knowledgeable. "I understand," he continued, apparently directing his next words to the attendant, "that those halls were originally colonnades, open to the air, and the rooms opening onto them had windows. The rooms were larger too and have been divided since."

"I would not know, sir. I only show visitors to their rooms."

Qala laughed. "Then lead us to ours! Hmm." She turned to Damana, carrying Zedos. "Do we put you with Horos?"

The girl shook her head. "Let him miss me a little."

"So cruel," commented Ranwif. "And my own sister!"

"You do know Ramapee and I might want our privacy," Qala told her. "So we need three rooms, as I know Ranwif has his own quarters in this pile of stone. One for Augun and Horos, and two for us girls and the child."

A faint smile from their guide. "Excellent, Lady Qala. That is what we had prepared."

He led them to the right, this time, at the top of the stairs. "By the way," Qala whispered to Ranwif, "just where are your quarters?"

Ranwif pointed up. "With the soldiers on the third floor. And there are windows." He chuckled. "Probably intended for shooting arrows from."

"You'll receive better if you join the service of the celos."

He sobered. "Undoubtedly. I think it's best but Domi likes being at Melawhem. With you, and near to Sesa."

"You'll work something out. These ones?" she asked the attendant. "Good enough." If he had hoped for a gratuity he had been mistaken. Qala had been here twice before. He should know by now.

"Then I'll leave you and go search out Lord Corad," said Ranwif. "I doubt the celos — it's going to take time to get used to that — will ask any of you to exert yourselves this evening."

"He'd best not," muttered Damana. Not that she was likely to be invited but she was protective of her mistress.

They had barely settled in when Ranwif returned, the heir of Sarowhem in tow. "Corad has all of the room he shared with Vullum to himself now so I'm going to move in," he said.

"Lord Vullum is to be on the ground floor. The king and queen plan a quiet private dinner this evening with him and his wife. Probably a bigger one for all of you tomorrow."

Queen, thought Qala. Queen Hasala. It was going to be harder to remember that than to call Flawum the celos. "Good with me," she said. "Why don't you run downstairs and get us something to eat, Corad?"

"As I would have two years ago? No need, Qala. Servants here obey me now." He stepped out but was gone only a couple minutes.

"Something will be brought up shortly," the nobleman announced. "Chances are they think it is for Vullum and I do not intend to inform them otherwise."

"So how goes the treaty-wrighting?"

"All forged and tempered. The work is done, unless some high-up Mur whispers in the emperor's ear at the last moment and changes his mind. That we can do nothing about."

"But the Viceroy is on your side." That man had his own whisperers, and men who preferred knives to lies, too.

"Indeed. He may have staked his career on this. None has more to lose if it fails, Flawum included. I hear someone in the hall. In here!" he called out. "We're all dining together."

"So his political opponents are another side to this. I should have thought of that." Qala was a bit angry with herself for it. She used to have a better grasp of intrigue. "But if it is delivered, signed, it is likely to be approved by the emperor himself." That man had far larger concerns than a semi-autonomous kingdom in the middle of nowhere.

"Almost certainly. If there is any more attempt to stop it, it will come soon. Most likely with action against Flawum himself, but maybe Murgom."

"Why not both?" asked Ranwif. "Where is our boy Horos? Across the hall?"

"Augun, too," said Damana. "Tell them to get over here."

"I have heard rumors of you and Horos," said Corad.

She beamed. "We are to be married! Soon, I hope. Aren't there priests in this place?"

"I can marry you," Ramapee told her, "as a priestess of Kamat."

"Oh!" Elation faded quickly. "Oh. Mom would want it at home. A priest of Jov, too."

"No reason you can not have two ceremonies," said Qala. "One now, one when we get home."

"Great! Oh, Horos," she cried as the boy entered. "I have really, reeeally, great, wonderful news!"

"I am sure you do," said her intended.

48.

"Gonna marry king's daughter," Zedos proclaimed.

The look Flawum gave him suggested he did not consider it such an unreasonable idea. Queen Hasala took it light-heartedly. "Have you decided which one, my dear? You would have to learn to tell the one from the other." She leaned over the crib. Maybe she was having trouble telling herself.

"Not *dese* daughters. Jong."

There it was. No keeping that from Flawum anymore. "And who is Jong?" he asked.

"Baby in udder world." Zedos sounded perplexed. He might have wanted to call the king a stupid-head.

"She has been here visiting," his wife told him. "Why — you don't you know about her, do you?"

"We thought it best he didn't," explained Qala. "No, the gods thought it best. I just went along."

"So one of those monsters had a child —"

It would be best to get the truth out. "All three of them." That would be news to both of them.

"Oh my," said the king, collapsing in an arm chair. "Oh my." He sat upright suddenly. "I should have known. I have obligations."

"It is likely you will never see the two of them," came Ramapee's quiet voice. "We are told they are bound to their world. Jong is another matter."

"I tow you," said Zedos, holding out a hand.

"No, Zedos! You are not taking the king to another world," cried his mother.

"Not one where demonesses desire his companionship," said Hasala. "From here out only I provide Flawum with children."

"Alright. I bring Jong sometime. Maybe Jong just gum all on by herself." Zedos seemed satisfied with that.

"She can do that?" whispered the queen.

"So it seems." Qala was not going to mention the idea she might be a god.

"We may need to add more rooms," jested Flawum. It fell a little flat, but he pushed on. "Speaking of rooms, I am seriously considering moving my capital south, at least during the cooler months. What thought you of Arlacas?"

"A horrible place," Qala told him. "Ridden with mosquitoes and disease, and built on mud that will swallow any substantial building."

"I agree," said Ramapee. "It is no place for your wife and children, your highness."

"Oh." He looked to his wife. "It seems you were right, my love."

Qala had what she considered a better idea. "There is a town one day's ride north from Arlacas that would make a far better capital. A good high bluff by the river, plenty of space to build, and away from the muck and stench of the river mouth."

"Hmm, and more central to my kingdom. I must speak to my advisors on this."

"Better to look it over yourself, sir," spoke Ramapee, "and advise them."

"Ha, indeed so." Flawum rose, so his guests did as well, not that he would stand on protocol. "I shall at least find it on a map this afternoon and maybe we can discuss it over dinner. You both are to come, of course. You, young man," he addressed Zedos, "must remain and make sure your nurse behaves."

"Send Horos udder world," he proclaimed and laughed at the idea. "Maybe mafadwi lige him too!"

"You'll do no such thing," scolded Ramapee, scooping him up. "Your highness," she nodded and left the nursery.

"Your son could be dangerous," said Flawum. Qala could not but agree. "This daughter. Is she, um, a monster?"

"More a rather homely lump of a little girl," stated his queen. "Large, too."

"That is her mafadwi form. Her monster form as you put it."

"Oh. Well enough. I shall see you this evening, my lady."

Qala was still weary from days on the road. She thought she might follow the Sharshite custom this day and take the siesta. That plan was not to be, not at once, for Lenco sat on one of the beds, conversing with Damana and Horos.

He turned his sleek dark head to the newcomers. "I should bring one of my priests here for the wedding," the god declared. "There are yet a few."

"Which wedding?" asked Qala. "We intend two ceremonies." Zedos ran to his uncle as soon as he was set on his feet.

"Either or both. Or perhaps you and Ramapee would like one too. Greetings, Zedos. Have you been taking care of them all?"

The boy only nodded and looked up at him. "You Looty daddy? Looty hide."

"Indeed I am, though the girl doesn't like to admit to it. And we are looking for her, never fear. Those jewels that pop up in all of this from time to time may help us."

"The Eyes of the Wind," said Qala.

"Also called the Jewels of the Elements," Ramapee added. "Known of old by our Ildin priesthoods."

"Yes, Banat's people held them for some time," said Lenco, "and Im stole them from their temple. At my brother's urging, to be sure, and to protect them."

"This I did not know," admitted the young woman.

"Doesn't matter much. They are together and an attempt will be made to use them. That is nothing for me to get involved in." His eyes went back to Zedos. "And neither should you, if you were thinking of it."

"Alright." The boy was too sleepy to raise an argument.

"We shall have to begin his education in earnest," said the lithe god, returning his attention to Qala. "When you get home and settled should be soon enough. My congratulations to both couples." Lenco snickered. "Though as a phallic deity you may guess to whom I give my blessings." With that he pulled shadow about himself and departed.

"We can have the wedding tomorrow morning," announced Ramapee. "Then off to home?"

"It is to be hoped," said Qala. Home. Ramapee called Melawhem home. "Now let me rest up a bit for this evening."

The same dress. It was the only one she brought and it did conceal her knives while making them readily accessible. She had made sure of that when ordering it. Qala fell asleep on that thought.

"What?" she sat up, fully awake. "Oh, Zedos. Finished with your nap too?"

"Uh-huh. Feel — feel Looty. Somewhere."

"That is good. Remember you promised your Uncle Lenco not to go looking."

"Yeah." He didn't sound too happy about it.

"But you need to go, my lady," said Damana. "Or get ready to go. It's growin' late."

"How can one tell in this place? It could be noon or midnight!" She should go find one of those hallways of windows. Not now. She would take the girl's word for it and get dressed.

Qala ended up sitting for some time before Corad appeared to escort her. And Ramapee, of course. Shouldn't she be Ramapee's escort, the one to enter Flawum's dining hall on her arm? She would make sure to do that when they arrived at the doors.

Ramapee, as ever, wore her priestess' red gown. I hope she changes sometimes when we get home, thought Qala. As it was, they were among the first guests so hardly anyone noted her gesture of entering with her love.

Not even the king and his wife. A noble couple of the court she did not know, servants, guards. The Sharshite pair seemed happy to not be the only guests any longer. Friends of the queen, they were, probably added to fill out the party. Qala would have found them exceptionally uninteresting save that there was nothing exceptional about them.

Vullum and Galana appeared soon. That should improve things but little ensued other than small talk. At last, the royal couple, and Admiral Murgom with them. And, at last, the wine would be poured.

Flawum raised a goblet in toast. "To the final and successful crafting of our treaty," he spoke. "A thank you to all of you who helped in your ways. That includes you, Domwif. Your private advice was invaluable."

The Sharshite nobleman nodded an acknowledgment. "Soon to be Thegn Domwif. Or I guess you already are, now the treaty has been signed." Flawum quaffed and sat. "That's a sign to bring the first course," he reminded the servants.

Some kind of soup? Why didn't they get right to the meat? Hmm,

Ramapee ate no meat. They would have to deal with that when they settled in at Melawhem. And what was that across the room, like a pool of — nothingness, edged with blood-red light, growing larger? It reminded her of the hole made by Ir when she had forced her way into this world.

At once, Qala was on her feet, a knife in her hand. "Stand ready," she cried, "and call more guards!" By now, most were staring at that same door between worlds as she. What was on its far side?

A beast-like snout came through, tusks and teeth, slobber dripping, steaming on the floor. Bristling red hair covered its semi-upright form. An ape? No, more a huge monkey. She could see its tail swinging back and forth behind it. Perhaps a form of demon, perhaps only a beast, but sent here to slay. That was certain.

It leaped toward them, no one individual seeming to be a target. The guardsmen moved to stay it, swords ready. Swords that seemed dreadfully inadequate to their task. How much less adequate would be Qala's knives! The men could not get inside the creatures long taloned arms. It tossed them aside, save one it decided to sample. One bite took away a third of the body.

The beast wrinkled its face in a most human way, showing its displeasure with the taste, and spat out the mangled remnant. Up it rose, up on it hind legs, and shrieked in anger. Spears were what were needed, thought Qala. Poke at it from a distance. Or better yet, run and be at an even greater distance. Ramapee should do that, at once. It surely intended to kill them all. As had whoever sent it.

"Get out," she rasped at the Ildin. "Run for it while it is distracted." Then she moved forward herself, picking up one of the scattered swords of the defenders. Was she surprised to see Flawum do the same? Galana was trying to herd the other women toward the door. No, Hasala pointed the other way. There must be an exit there. If only more men showed up! Enough of them might stop this beast, despite its strength and ferocity. None at the door, but surely coming. Make it soon or they would find only bodies.

Lord Domwif hurtled one of the heavy chairs toward it. The man must be stronger than he looked. It annoyed the beast, distracted it long enough for a man to slip in and deliver a sword thrust. He would never deliver another. Then — ah, then things changed as Qala never would have expected. It picked up two swords itself, one in each hand, and swung them expertly, advancing again.

How could such a creature be defeated?

49.

A near-deafening battle challenge rose behind her, a dark figure leaped forward, scooping up a pair of swords without pausing. A second later, fierce battle ensued between the monkey-monster and a muscular young woman. Lutanawa?

Yes, surely. Could anyone be that good a swordsman? Swordswoman, that was. No mortal, nor would Qala have believed it even of one divine. She sped forward to the attack herself. If Looty kept the monster busy maybe one of them could get in a damaging thrust. And there were more soldiers now, at the doors, to help. This attack was defeated, even if the creature itself were not.

There, someone got a blade in. Domwif again? Then one of Lutanawa's thrusts went home. The great muzzle raised itself and howled toward the ceiling. Of a sudden, the beast whirled about and loped back to its doorway, leaping through into the darkness beyond. It shut of a sudden, as silently as it had opened.

"Was that a mafadwi?" asked Flawum.

"No. That is no creature of my world," answered the glistening naked warrioress who had appeared in his dining hall.

"It looked somewht like one of the baboons of the southlands, sire," spoke Domwif. "But far, far larger."

"And better with a sword," commented Qala. "Your highness, may I present the Lady Lutanawa?"

"I give you my welcome and my thanks, my lady."

The goddess looked him over. "Jong's dad, right? Can't stop to talk. Need to go tell some of my relatives about this! They had just called me back and undoubtedly wonder where I disappeared to."

"You do have a way of disappearing," said Galana. She had slipped back into the room. Ramapee was there too. Had she ever left at all?

"Well said! I'll be back." Lutanawa disappeared again, in a jumble of disorienting images. She hadn't bothered to bring shadow about her to hide it, as was normal for her family.

"So much for my dinner party," said the king. "Better we discuss all this tomorrow. Oh, and I do intend to be there for the wedding in the morning." With that he passed out through the back way, in the wake of his queen.

"I'm still hungry," complained Qala.

Corad nodded agreement. "There is probably a stack of food in the kitchen that was intended to come here."

"I propose a raid. Do you wish to plunder the kitchens with us, Murgom?"

"I'll let the servants tend to it. Let's go talk about things Vullum." The nobleman could only give his wife an apologetic look and a shrug, before following the admiral from the room.

"So I'm with your raiding party," declared Lady Galana. "Our young goddess is quite deadly without becoming a snake at all, isn't she?"

"Young as goddesses go. Still far older than any of us can understand."

They left it to Corad to order part of the aborted royal banquet be delivered to Qala's room, and then proceeded to that room.

An empty room. Damana must have Zedos next door. She'd best not have Horos there too. No, it was empty as well. She rapped on the men's door. "Oh, you're back early, my lady," spoke Damana, opening it to them. "I'm tryin' to convince Horos he needs a bachelor party."

"And we're to give it," said Ranwif, giving Augun a slap on the back. Both had apparently started their party already.

"Only one bachelor party is allowed," Qala told them. "Now would you prefer it be here or back at Melawhem before the second ceremony?"

"Here," said Horos without hesitation.

"There!" shouted both Augun and Ranwif.

"Yeah, there's better," agreed Damana. "Benaro will want to have his part in it."

Zedos had wrapped his arms about her legs. "Mommy alright?" he asked.

"I am, thanks to your cousin Looty. Let's you and me go have our own party," she said, lifting him into her arms.

"No sense in me stayin' here," said Damana, and followed them.

"We shall all need to get our rest if the wedding is at dawn," spoke Ramapee. "Do you think your king will actually get up that early?"

"He always does, these days," Corad informed her. "Will it be outdoors?"

"It doesn't have to be. We just need to see the rising sun. I figured we'd go out in the courtyard."

"Not the best of views, what with the walls around it. Follow me." He led them back toward the wider east-west hall onto which the main stairway opened but turned to the left, away from those stairs. At the end, to both sides, ran a window-lined hallway. All those windows would face the sun come morning. "There's an alcove of sorts down that way," said Corad, gesturing to the right. "I sometimes bring my breakfast down here."

"Perfect!" declared Damana. "Don't you think so, Zedos?"

"Perfect," he repeated.

"And by now, food might be arriving at your rooms. Let's go eat."

"Perfect," said Zedos.

It took no time at all for Augun and Ranwif to smell out a feast and join them. There was plenty of the mediocre strong wine to which they had become accustomed here, the product of the wide, sun-drenched plains of northern Lorj. Qala was wondering if she had room for another sweet-cake.

"Sorry I'm late. Anything left?"

"Loooooty!" cried out Zedos.

The goddess was dressed somewhat more appropriately now. That is, she wore clothes. But they were what she wore in her own home, a loin-cloth and no more. She would need to learn a few things if she kept visiting mortals.

Xido coalesced out of shadow at her side. "We're only here for a few minutes," he said.

"You are, my uncle. I might decide to stick around."

"As you will. I may pop back tomorrow anyway. What happened this evening raises all sorts of questions."

"The Cana doesn't like him away from her bed too long," snickered the goddess.

"Which is none of your business, Lutanawa. I hope my son doesn't pick up your bad manners."

This was not going well. "So how did you find your way back, Looty?" asked Qala. "The last I saw, you were slithering after Quso."

"Whom I caught at the water's edge. I took a while with him. You know, letting my venom do its work, breaking him up a little to make him easier to swallow. What, shouldn't I say that?"

"Maybe not," Xido replied, his tone much gentler now. He's recognizing her 'bad manners' are largely ignorance, Qala thought. And a certain native rambunctiousness, not unlike her father. How many times had she heard his sister scold him for that sort of thing?

"Very well. By the time I got him down, it seemed all the fight had gone out of those pirates — though they were still an argumentative bunch — and you were gone. And I was full and sleepy so I slipped off to lie up a while. Not that I was actually thinking things out like that, except dimly with my snake mind."

"Well do I understand that," muttered Xido.

"And I don't believe I was thinking at all when I woke up a couple days later. That's the risk when we change form in another world."

"At home, we transition from one to the other readily, most of the time," her uncle added. "So we knew we were going to have to look for her and try to jolt her out of it, if we could. Me and Saj and Kataree, all together in Lanlaz, and Im at a distance, sharing the power of the Eyes. Not the full power, not entering them, of course, just what was needed to find an elusive snake."

"They could have let things take their course. I would have come back eventually."

"We felt it best. Saj is good at finding things, you know, especially near the sea. Just lots of practice, most likely. We discovered a sleepy cobra sunning on a ledge not far from where you left her. No telling what meal she had just swallowed."

"I've no idea," said Lutanawa. "Nothing has any taste in that form. It's just swallow and sleep and digest. By Krat himself, I am glad you brought me back! As soon as I returned to this form, I popped myself home to my own house."

"Are you ready to return to your home again?"

"For a time, for a time. But I will come back to my new friends here.

And," she stated, "I think I should go visit Im soon. It was his voice that brought me home."

50.

"Now the king knows where this is taking place?"

"I told him myself, young lady," Galana told her.

"A king at our weddin', Horos. Isn't that grand?"

"Qala is good enough for me," the boy maintained.

"Oh, to be sure. Lady Qala's better'n any king."

The Lady Galana turned her attention to Ramapee and Qala. "I could give you two a ceremony as a priestess of Esefa. Let me know."

"I don't need a ceremony," whispered Ramapee, taking Qala's hand. But it would certainly flatter the goddess. They could always use extra blessings and divine goodwill. Maybe when they got home. Maybe in the shrine she had promised to build.

"There's Flawum." No queen with him. Lord Vullum had declined to show as well, but Murgom rolled along at the king's side. That was a pretty good addition to the list of wedding guests. And Corad was here, and Ranwif and Augun.

She mustn't forget the smallest guest, either. Zedos may not have grasped all that was going on but he knew something good was happening to those he loved. Qala suspected he did grasp more than most his age would. But she also knew mothers tended to do that sort of thing.

There was sunlight, dawn showing at the tall, narrow windows. So much glass! More than she had ever seen in one building, that was for sure. There must have been great wealth in the days of the last Sharshite kings.

And to think she had missed this view all the days she had stayed here. Ramapee had stepped forward and begun, in lilting Ildin. The kids wouldn't mind that they couldn't understand her. As in the ceremonies at home, there were crowns of leaves to be placed on each other's heads. Was that a borrowing from the Ildin?

Now the priestess had switched to Sharshic, instructing the pair in their married duties, announcing them man and wife. "Yay!" called out Zedos. Then the boy stopped, as if listening to something, his face serious. "Jong gum," he said, and a moment later Flawum's daughter took form.

Hasala had been discreet when she described the girl as homely. Jong's form was thick, blocky, the face sullen, its features heavy, somehow alien.

"Dada?" It was the first word Qala had heard her speak. She reached up toward Flawum. Flawum recoiled a little, despite himself.

The little mafadwi stopped. Two images formed, pulled apart from each other, contracted together again. Jong was struggling to control them. All at once, only one remained, an extremely pretty little girl. Large, to be sure, but all the grossness of her form was gone. Then it snapped back. The girl stamped her large foot in anger and disappeared.

"Mafadwi Jong gum back," remarked Zedos, then turned to Flawum. "King mean to her! Bad daddy!" The boy seemed quite angry.

"I know," the man admitted. "I didn't mean to make her go. Please tell her I am sorry." There was even a tear in his eye. Qala doubted not a moment he meant it.

But there was a more important matter. Jong could divide her natures, and at an early age. The third requirement, at least in Mawa's eyes, for being a god.

"Go," said Zedos, and disappeared. Off to console Jong, she assumed. Qala did not even feel the need to worry about it anymore. Well, a little, to be sure.

"Do we wait for him?" asked Damana.

"No. He'll come when he's ready. And breakfast is waiting. "

"How does breakfast wait?" someone asked. "Does it go stand on the corner? Oh, I missed it all, didn't I?"

"We did not expect you, Looty."

"I'm goin' to have another one in a little while," Damana told her. "You're invited."

"I thank you. Where's Zedos?"

"I'll explain." First, they must be pleasant to Flawum and Murgom, thank them for coming, exchange small talk. It ended quickly. Flawum was in a hurry to go, upset about his encounter with Jong. Murgom might well have stayed for breakfast but decided to trail after the king. Flawum had not even commented on Lutanawa's appearance.

She was more modestly attired this morning, by the standards of this land and this world. Someone had talked to her or maybe she just noticed things. Qala let her know what had just happened with Jong as they followed the married couple back to the rooms.

"It surprises me not at all," said Lutanawa. "Dividing oneself is essentially the same process as moving from world to world. We gods send our two halves to different worlds. Our beast natures, mmm, sleep, but we are always joined, ready to call on their power."

"Your relatives will want to know about this."

"No doubt. Maybe I'll tell them. Would you like me to go fetch your runaway boy?"

Why not? "Certainly, Looty. Maybe you can even say something to Jong. Oh, I didn't mention she spoke her first word."

"It's nice she can do more than sing. She does not look at all like a bird. Hmm." The goddess drifted off in a thought for a moment. "I would like to know what her other form is like now. Her beast form."

"Maybe like a Sharshite Ancient? Esefa called them great, ugly giants."

"She's prejudiced, but some of them are, to be sure. Maybe her other nature is like that."

"But her singing comes from your world."

"The song of Krat is all around her, around all of us, but she has heard it more clearly. Maybe we shut it out. I'll go see what the boy is up to." With that she faded away, this time politely covering the process with shadow.

It was midmorning when they were called to council with the celos. Lutanawa had not returned with her son, and there was naught to do about that. A different god waited in the chamber, already in conference with Flawum.

"I thought I should speak here," said Xido. "I have learned things recently and put other things together. I and the Cana and others."

Others were slipping in but Flawum paid them little mind. "The great question is why we were attacked with sorcery last night. Who would do such a thing?"

"The 'who' is simple. Dxukur, the Wizard-Lord himself, who had an alliance of sorts with the pirates. Now, the Wizard-Lord had no particular incentive to put himself in service of the Pirate King, other than to take possession of certain valuable magical artifacts."

"The Eyes. You have told me all about them."

Xido had to smile at that. "Hardly all, my lord. That fell through and they are beyond his reach. For now."

"Good," said Flawum. He held up a hand when a servant approached with a wine jug. "All servants out," he ordered. "Only those invited remain." Turning back to the god, he said, "So that was the basis of the alliance with the pirates. But why would he help work against the treaty?"

"His goal all along is political sabotage. He hopes to weaken the empire, here, there, and be able to dominate the Old Kingdoms across the Great Sea. He has probed and been pushed back more than once."

"That be so," stated Murgom. "If you're not going to have any of that wine, slide the jug over here."

"In time, he may hope to control the Mura here as well, destroy or conquer the empire. His ambition is boundless and his power great. Believe, mortals," he said, looking up and down the table, "a great conflict will come. This past century Dxukur has been content with building his power at home and feeling things out."

"And my little kingdom matters in all this?"

"An enemy south of the Muram Empire is better than a friend. Poverty and disruption of trade is preferable to prosperity. All adds up. Long-lived wizards can play such a game."

It was Vullum who broke the following silence. "What do we do?"

"You have done it. Your treaty is a setback for the Wizard-Lord. All of this has been. Peace will come, for a time, and that time may allow some to better prepare. There is no other course."

"Then we can ride for home. Or be carried." The nobleman gave a sidelong look to the admiral.

"So you can," agreed Flawum. "I am certain you have seen too much of these walls. But," he said, returning to Xido, "whence came that beast that attacked us?"

"I have not the slightest idea. Believe it or not, your highness, there are worlds even I have not seen."

51.

"My daughter. Why does she have that look? It is nothing like her mother, but it is not — human."

Xido nodded to Qala, so she gave the answer. "Yet it comes from you. You know the tale of an ancestress bearing the child of an Ancient One, do you not?"

Flawum nodded. He had asked the two to stay after the conference, apparently to discuss this matter.

"That blood is in you and it has come to the ascendant in your daughter."

"So it was a true tale — but none of my ancestors ever looked like that!"

Now Xido it was who spoke. "For they were mortals, born of mortals, in this world. It would have remained hidden."

"Jong will learn to become human. She has shown she is able." That seemed pretty certain to Qala.

"She will be taught. But —" Xido at a loss for words? "She is not mortal. Jong is a goddess. There is no other way to put it. She does not belong to your world, Flawum, though she may come to love it and love you."

Does she belong to Xido's world? wondered Qala. To the world of Krat?

"And to love my son," he continued. "My son who is a mortal. And who is on his way — here." Zedos popped into the room, Lutanawa following.

"I hope I have smoothed things over with Jong," she announced. "Me and Zedos. Her feelings were hurt but she is awfully young. Just be nice next time, huh?"

"That I shall, my lady. I hope there is a next time."

"I would count on it." She sat down, peered into a jug of wine and then drained it. "So, Uncle Xit — Xit, I like that. I shall use it from now on. Anyway, so I've talked it over with your siblings — yes, even my father — and they think I should teach Zedos. Mostly because I volunteered!"

The dark god raised an eyebrow. "Jong too?"

"Oh, no. This will free up Uncle Budo to concentrate on her. Not that we won't switch off or combine classes and do other teacher stuff. But with the two of them in different worlds it makes sense for each to have a dedicated instructor. If her mother doesn't mind me moving in." She turned her eyes to Qala. "Or at least having the occasional long visit."

"His tutor. I could do worse."

"We could do worse," said Xido. "We all part at dawn? I back to the Cana and her mission, you north, the new celos to buckle down to the governing of his realm."

"I may give advice occasionally," stated Qala.

"And I may listen to it," answered Flawum. "You didn't drink all the wine, did you Lady Lutawahwah and I'm sure I got that wrong."

"Call me Looty. I'm handy with advice too. Hmm, there's some sloshing about in this jug." She handed it up the table. "And don't you sample it, Zedos. I know you're too young."

"Budo served him beer when he was an infant," admitted Qala, "when nothing else was to be had. It seemed to do no harm."

"Budo beer! Yummmy, yummy, fill my tummy!"

"He may have sampled it since," said Xido.

There was leave-taking that evening, but no feast. Best to get started early and clear-headed. North they rode at dawn, toward the River Chas, toward Melawhem. Qala wondered where exactly the new official border lay. Did Flawum get his thirty leagues or was it twenty?

Progress was pinned to the speed of Murgom's horse litter and his foot-soldiers, which meant a leisurely trip. Would it be bad manners to ditch them and ride ahead with her own little entourage? Qala wanted to be home. She wanted to be home badly.

Near noon, that first day, Looty lifted her head suddenly. "There is a place of power near us."

"A gate. I passed through it once with, um, with your father."

"Ah, then it is the way Im first came to this world. He wasn't born here, you know." Qala didn't but let the goddess continue.

"All the memories he aroused in me are what brought back my other side. It is that part of me that makes me human, isn't it? We gods are human, you know, even if we aren't mortal." She snickered. "Partly human. I will go visit Im but not right away. First I ride north with you, like a human, and see this world. I will approach your manor as you approach it, see it as you see it."

"Zedos will not be the only one to learn."

"Even so, Qala."

Qala amused herself over the following days with picking out good spots to build a tavern or inn. Had her agent looked into the ownership of any of this land? For that matter, who owned the property along Chas between her estate and that of Lord Hurrum? It was not a long stretch but it never seemed to have been developed.

Their road led them into Melawhem from the southeast, winding through fields and barns and cottages before reaching the manor house and hall. Lutanawa took this in with some interest, chattering questions about this and that, many most elementary. Qala thought perhaps Ramapee was seeing the place with a new eye. Perhaps she was herself.

"If you see a spot you like for a shrine to Kamat, let me know," she told her. She herself was considering different sites for Esefa's shrine.

"Kamat doesn't really need shrines," Ramapee said, but added with a slight smile, "He *is* fond of high places. None too many of those here."

"Maybe we need to visit that cave in the hills. But that was Banat's shrine, wasn't it?"

"So it was. There is Domi, coming to greet us."

52.

Lord Hurrum was settled in at Melawhem, as was his daughter-in-law. "They hurried here as soon as news came north of Lady Galana's rescue," Domi told her, "and didn't go."

"We'll bundle all of them off to Sarowhem as soon as we are able," Qala promised. "But you will have new faces to replace theirs. That one," she said, nodding in Lutanawa's direction, "you will make known as Zedos's cousin Looty."

"Luti. Very well. And she's going to stay?"

"Probably longer than you. She is his tutor. That can and should be known too. I suspect the news has already reached your ears that Damana and Horos are married. We should have another wedding here, as soon as convenient."

"Indeed yes. Who'd have thought it?"

"Oh, I planned this entire adventure just to bring them together."

"Yes, Qala, of course. And Ramapee came back without her mistress? The Lady Lura didn't come to harm, did she?"

"The Cana is fine. Ramapee has decided to be with me."

"A secretary? She's good with a pen. I noticed."

"More than a secretary. More than any job."

"Ah. That is good but make her do some work too! I don't let Ranwif loaf, you know. By the way, I am glad you brought him back with you."

"Though I know you will both leave, sooner or later. Has he had a chance to tell you Flawum made him a knight? No? Just before we left, in the morning as we were readying the horses, he hurried out of his keep and went through the ceremony. With all that had been going on, I think it slipped his mind!"

"Better late than never *is* a proverb," said Domi.

"And he'll be more soon, count on it. Arlacana holds the future for him, Domi. For you too."

"I know. But I won't go until after the baby comes. This I have decided."

"I think it a wise decision. Now what is your father up to?"

The nobleman stood before the group of arrivals, looking for someone, it seemed. He went to Augun, motioned him forward. "I must speak to the man-at-arms Augun before all else," proclaimed Lord Hurrum. "Some suspected you of treachery, sir, but the message my son sent north changed that. We looked into doings of the cook Lovi and found enough there to question him. He admitted he had passed some news to a spy of the Pirate King and further that the spy was a wizard, sending the information on from afar. He also told us where the man hid. The wizard we hung. Lovi we spared for his cooperation, but banished." The nobleman placed a hand on the former pirate's shoulder. "I am sorry of this, Augun."

"Lord Hurrum may have spared him the gallows but if he ever showed up around here again, I'd be the one slitting his throat," growled Augun.

"I'm sorry of losing his cooking," put in Corad. "I hope he taught his assistants a little something."

"His best student is right here," spoke Qala. "Let's get him to fix us something."

As the road wound around the west side of the manor house before ending at the ferry, they must go across the lawn to the hall. All trailed behind Qala, with Ramapee at her side. Both Domi and Ranwif had disappeared, probably attending to all the chores associated with the arrival of new guests, stabling, lodging, feeding. She would miss having them here.

"Lady Galana," she called, "I think Esefa would like a shrine near the water. What say you to that spot over there?"

"On the stream? Perfect."

"And you must return for the dedication. And for more." She halted there, putting her arms around the woman she loved, forgetting all the others.

"For so much more," she whispered.

Afterword

Qala the Pirate Queen was first introduced as a secondary character in my novel, *The Eyes of the Wind*, and was just too interesting not to follow up in a semi-sequel, *The Crocodile's Son*. This is the sequel to that book and probably the last in which Qala will have the lead role. We definitely leave her with a happy ending and I think that should stick.

The Baxac gods I introduce here are very loosely based on Melanesian mythology. This makes sense as the Baxac people are supposed to have a similar origin. There are a great many variations on the legends and gods of the Melanesian peoples so I took my share of liberties in creating this pantheon.

The tales of Qala and Zedos, told in the two Crocodile Chronicles novels (*The Crocodile's Son*, *The Crocodile God*) are interwoven with those of Saj and Marana in the two Sajam Saga novels (*The Eyes of the Wind*, *The Jewels of the Elements*), making one story but each book able to stand on its own.

A final note: though one is generally safe pronouncing Muram and Sharshic words and names like Spanish, those from the Ildin language are another matter. The accent often falls on the first syllable, as in Ramapee's name.

Stephen Brooke

Author Stephen Brooke lives in an old farmhouse in the Florida Panhandle. He is the author of more than twenty books, as well as an artist and musician.

Visit the Arachis Press at http://arachispress.com for more of his work.

www.ingramcontent.com/pod-product-compliance
Lightning Source LLC
Chambersburg PA
CBHW030326020726
47493CB00004B/1173